PUFFIN BOOKS

Judi Curtin

Double Trouble

D1323974

Judi was born in London and grew up in Cork. She now lives in Limerick with her family. She has three children and a cat called Domino. Domino does not have any superpowers – as far as she knows. In her spare time, Judi likes to read, play Scrabble and grow tomatoes.

Books by Judi Curtin

FRIENDS FOREVER: THE TIME SPELL
FRIENDS FOREVER: DOUBLE TROUBLE

Double Trouble

JUDI CURTIN

Illustrated by Sara Flavell

PUFFIN

PUFFIN BOOKS

Published by the Penguin Group
Penguin Books Ltd, 80 Strand, London WC2R 0RL, England
Penguin Group (USA) Inc., 375 Hudson Street, New York, New York 10014, USA
Penguin Group (Canada), 90 Eglinton Avenue East, Suite 700, Toronto, Ontario, Canada M4P 2Y3
(a division of Pearson Penguin Canada Inc.)
Penguin Ireland, 25 St Stephen's Green, Dublin 2, Ireland (a division of Penguin Books Ltd)
Penguin Group (Australia), 250 Camberwell Road, Camberwell, Victoria 3124, Australia
(a division of Pearson Australia Group Pty Ltd)
Penguin Books India Pvt Ltd, 11 Community Centre, Panchsheel Park, New Delhi – 110 017, India
Penguin Group (NZ), 67 Apollo Drive, Rosedale, Auckland 0632, New Zealand
(a division of Pearson New Zealand Ltd)
Penguin Books (South Africa) (Pty) Ltd, 24 Sturdee Avenue, Rosebank, Johannesburg 2196, South Africa

Penguin Books Ltd, Registered Offices: 80 Strand, London WC2R 0RL, England

puffinbooks.com

First published 2012

1

Text copyright © Judi Curtin, 2012
Illustrations by Sara Flavell © Puffin Books
All rights reserved

The moral right of the author and illustrator has been asserted

Set in 13/20 pt Baskerville MT Standard
Typeset by Palimpsest Book Production Limited, Falkirk, Stirlingshire
Printed in Great Britain by Clays Ltd, St Ives plc

British Library Cataloguing in Publication Data
A CIP catalogue record for this book is available from the British Library

ISBN: 978–0–141–33511–7

www.greenpenguin.co.uk

MIX
Paper from
responsible sources
FSC
www.fsc.org   FSC™ C018179

Penguin Books is committed to a sustainable
future for our business, our readers and our
planet. This book is made from paper certified
by the Forest Stewardship Council.

For Dan, Brian, Ellen and Annie

1

'I can't believe it,' I said. 'I just can't believe it.'

'It's not all that bad,' said Tilly.

'Of course it's that bad. We work really hard all week, and then Mrs Simms announces that we've got to spend the whole weekend doing a history project. That so isn't fair.'

'Look on the bright side. We're allowed to work in pairs, and Mrs Simms said we can work on any history topic that interests us.'

'But what if there's no history topic that interests me so much that I'd want to spend a whole weekend working on it?'

'You could try explaining that to Mrs Simms on Monday?'

1

I shook my head. 'No way. She'd kill me.'

'The project won't seem like such a big deal once we've done the first bit. Come on – let's go over to your place and we can get started.'

I knew she was right, but that really didn't make me feel any better.

When we got to my house, I could hear loud voices coming from an open upstairs window. It was my mum and my big sister Amy having one of their daily shouting matches.

I groaned and made a face at Tilly.

'Don't make me go in there,' I said. 'They'll want me to take sides. I'll do my best, but no matter what I do, in an hour's time, Mum and Amy will be best friends again, and they'll both be cross with me.'

'Let's sit out here for a while then,' said Tilly, flinging herself on to the bench on the green outside my house.

As I sat next to her, I wriggled free of my schoolbag and flung it on to the grass. I wished that I'd never have to see it again.

On the other side of the green, my little brother, Stephen, and his friends were playing soccer.

After a few minutes, my cat Saturn appeared from the bushes and came to cuddle in my arms.

'I still think he's the most beautiful cat I've ever seen,' said Tilly.

I couldn't argue with her – Saturn is amazing. He's a Turkish Angora cat, with silky white fur and the most incredible mismatched eyes, one blue and the other green.

'Guess what, Lauren,' said Tilly, as she stroked Saturn's soft fur. 'I have a secret.'

I smiled. I love hearing secrets. 'Well – out with it.'

Tilly shook her head. 'No. I started this, so you have to tell me a secret first.'

'But I haven't got any secrets,' I protested. 'I tell you everything.'

Suddenly I noticed that Saturn was staring at me. I love Saturn deeply, but sometimes he scares me a bit.

Sometimes I feel he knows what's going on inside my head.

And while most cats probably only think about

saucers of milk and rooms full of fat, lame mice, I had a weird feeling that Saturn was thinking of something else.

He jumped out of my arms and went to lie in the shade nearby. He still stared at me, though, and I couldn't help feeling that his huge odd eyes were accusing me.

You see, I did have a secret. I had a very, very big secret. And I had often thought of sharing it with Tilly.

But it was too big. It was too incredible.

But now Tilly was looking at me too, as if she was waiting for me to say something. And she has these piercing, pale blue eyes, and when she stares at me like that, I start to feel really nervous. And she is my very, very best friend.

So I started to talk.

Much, much later, I realized that Tilly hadn't interrupted once, which sooo isn't like her. She twiddled with her hair the way she always does when she's trying to figure something out.

4

'Please say something,' I said, when the silence became too much for me.

Tilly took a deep breath. 'Let me get this straight. You're telling me that Saturn has strange powers and that he dragged you back to the past; and that you spent days and days there, even though no time passed here; and that you made friends with all these people who are dead now; and that you ended up on the *Titanic* and managed to escape just before it sank, and . . . you expect me to believe you?'

'Well, actually, yes.'

'Have you got any proof?'

I sighed. Tilly has a very logical mind. For her, everything is about proof.

I thought for a minute. There had to be a way of convincing Tilly that I was telling the truth. But Tilly is smart. She wouldn't be fooled by me getting a chunk of ice from the freezer and telling her it was part of the iceberg that sank the *Titanic*.

She was going to need real proof.

There was the medal that one of my friends from 1912 had given me – but I could have found that lying in the street, or picked it up in an antique shop.

There was the fact that I know heaps of stuff about the *Titanic* – but I could have found all that out on the Internet.

And there was my old fleece, which ended up in a photograph that was taken in the 1930s – but that photo was far away in a little village near Cork.

I knew I was wasting my time. I could hardly believe this crazy story myself, so how on earth could I expect Tilly to believe it?

I was starting to feel sorry that I'd mentioned it.

'This isn't working, Lauren,' said Tilly in the end. 'I know you made this whole thing up, so you might as well be honest and admit it.'

'You're right,' I said quickly. 'I just made it up. Good story, though, wasn't it?'

She grinned. 'Great story. That's why you always get such high marks for your English essays – you've got a great imagination. Now will I tell you my secret?'

I'd managed to forget all about Tilly's secret.

'Go ahead,' I said.

Tilly went slightly red, and then she whispered, 'There's this guy who's moved into a house near me, and he's really kind of cute.'

I laughed. 'That's it? That's your big secret?'

'OK, so it's not a brilliant secret, but at least it's true. Not like your makey-uppy time-travel story.'

I knew I'd hurt her, and I felt bad.

'I'm sorry, Tilly,' I said. 'That's a great secret. Why don't I call over to your place tomorrow, and maybe we can get to know this guy?'

She put her arm round me. 'Thanks, Lauren,' she said.

Just then Saturn jumped into Tilly's arms. She stroked him and he purred loudly.

'Your house has gone quiet,' said Tilly. 'Maybe it's safe to go inside and get started on that project.'

I nodded and stood up to go inside. I stopped suddenly, though, as Tilly cried out. I could see that Saturn was shaking like a small leaf in a very big storm.

'Shhh, Saturn,' I said softly. 'It's OK.'

I bent down to rub him, but he just continued to shake in Tilly's arms as he stared at the blank patch of grass in front of us.

Saturn had only behaved like this once before.

I started to feel very, very afraid.

'Tilly, I think we'd better . . .' I began to say, but I couldn't finish the sentence.

There was a familiar blinding light and a loud, loud noise. It was like a disco scene from a bad horror movie. I reached for Tilly's hand and held it tightly.

Tilly, I wanted to say. *You have to be brave. Things are going to get very weird very soon.*

But how can you say anything when your cheeks are rattling and your eyeballs feel like they are going to pop out?

So I closed my eyes as tightly as I could and hoped for the best.

 2

When I opened my eyes, I was sitting on a dusty road that ran between two fields. Tilly was sitting next to me, using one hand to rub her eyes and the other to cling on to Saturn. Tilly's schoolbag was on her back, but there was no sign of mine. I had a horrible feeling that it was still on the grass in front of our house.

I stood up and looked around. For as far as I could see, there were only fields and more fields – but they weren't fields like I'm used to. These were cracked, dry, yellow fields, and when I stared at them I thought I could see the air above them shimmering in the heat.

'Where are we?' whispered Tilly.

'I have no idea,' I whispered back, wondering why we both felt the need to be so quiet.

'And how did we get here?'

I had the benefit of experience. I pointed at Saturn, who was lazily licking his lips.

'I'm thinking that Saturn brought us here. I told you he has magical powers.'

'But you made all that stuff up. You even admitted that it was just a story.'

I ignored her.

'Saturn's probably brought us back in time,' I said.

'Time travel is impossible,' said Tilly. 'I accept that something strange has happened, and we don't seem to be sitting in front of your house any more, but there has to be a logical explanation.'

I looked around and tried to figure things out. We were in the middle of the countryside, with no buildings to guide us, but still I was fairly sure that we weren't in the twenty-first century.

'This has to be the past,' I said in the end. 'There are no telephone lines and no electrical masts. There's no sound of cars or any other kind of engines. Look up, Tilly. Why are there no planes, or white jet trails in the sky?'

'Maybe because we're in the future? Maybe we've skipped forward to the twenty-fifth century and all the telephone lines are invisible. Maybe cars are so fast we can't see or hear them, and jets don't leave trails in the sky any more.'

'Wow! Do you really think so?'

She made a face. 'No, Lauren, I don't think so. Like I said, time travel doesn't make any sense. It's impossible. I don't know where exactly we are, but I know it's still Friday. And the date is still the same as the one I wrote at the top of my homework diary half an hour ago.'

Then I thought of something else.

'Look at my phone,' I said, reaching for my schoolbag. Then I remembered that my phone and my schoolbag were still on the grass at home.

'Oh,' I said. 'I think my phone might be very far away from here. Have you got yours?'

Tilly opened her schoolbag and took out her phone.

'Try calling someone,' I said.

Tilly shook her head. 'I can't. I don't seem to have a signal.'

'You see,' I said. 'That proves it. We've gone back in time.'

Tilly shook her head. 'All that proves is that we seem to be somewhere remote – very remote.'

I sighed. 'Why can't you just believe me, Tilly? It's like I told you. Saturn can go back in time. Last time he brought me, and this time he's brought both of us. I know it's scary but –'

'It's not scary because it's not true,' Tilly interrupted. 'Like I said before, there has to be a logical explanation. We seem to be in some faraway place, and we need to find someone who can give us a lift home, that's all.'

I felt a sudden burst of anger.

'When I last travelled back in time, I was scared at first because I was on my own,' I said. 'But with you here, everything could be different. This could be an amazing adventure for the two of us, but you're spoiling it because you won't believe what's happening right in front of you.'

As I spoke, I could feel my eyes filling up with tears.

Tilly stood up and hugged me, squashing Saturn between us. 'I don't want to fight with you, Lauren,' she said. 'But you're not a baby. I can't pretend to believe something just to keep you happy.'

'Don't believe it to make me happy,' I said. 'Believe it because it's true.'

She hesitated. 'How about you believe what you want, and I'll believe what I want, and then we'll see what happens?'

I wiped my eyes and nodded. I knew she'd believe me in the end. It was only a matter of time.

Just then, Saturn jumped out of Tilly's arms and began to walk along the road.

'Should we follow him?' asked Tilly.

I shrugged. 'I don't really know.'

'Well, you're supposed to be the expert. What did you do the last time you *time-travelled*?'

She used her fingers to mime quotation marks round *time-travelled*.

'I know you're mocking me, Tilly,' I said. 'And I

don't care. And, for your information, last time I did follow Saturn.'

'And?'

'And I ended up on the *Titanic*.'

'That sounds like fun,' said Tilly, giggling. 'Ending up on a ship that's about to sink into the icy ocean.'

I had to giggle too. 'Well, it wasn't exactly fun at first, but it all turned out OK in the end.'

'So we follow Saturn, that's the rule?'

'I don't know anything about rules. It's just that if we lose Saturn, I have a funny feeling that we'll never get back home.'

'So what are we waiting for?' said Tilly as she started to run. 'Come on, Lauren. Last one to Saturn is a dirty rotten time traveller.'

We soon caught up with Saturn and for a while we walked slowly along the road after him. The sun was shining and it was really hot. I wished I was wearing shorts and a T-shirt instead of my warm, scratchy school uniform.

'I am so thirsty,' said Tilly for the hundredth time. 'I hope we come to a shop or a restaurant soon.'

I sighed. 'We have no idea where or when we are. Maybe shops don't exist in this time and place.'

Tilly rolled her eyes and didn't reply.

Much later, we were sitting in the shade of a tree. Saturn was perfectly relaxed, curled up in a ball beside us. I was just about to drop off to sleep when I heard the distant sound of horses' hooves. Tilly jumped to her feet.

'At last!' she said. 'We're rescued. We'll be back home before we know it.'

Suddenly I felt uneasy.

'Tilly?'

'What?'

'What if the people here aren't nice? What if we've landed in a place where everyone is mean and vicious?'

'Saturn wouldn't bring us to a place like that, would you, Saturn?'

Saturn looked up at the sound of his name and stared at us for a minute. Then he rested his head on his paws and closed his eyes.

As the sound of the hooves came closer, my heart started to beat faster.

Tilly picked up her schoolbag and dusted off her clothes. I wondered why she wasn't scared. Was she incredibly brave? Or incredibly foolish?

'Maybe we should hide,' I said, but it was too late. Round the bend came two huge horses pulling a big chariot-like thing behind them. On the chariot were two men and a boy of about fifteen. All three were wearing knee-length dresses, which might have looked funny, except that I was in no mood for laughing.

Saturn gave a whimper and scuttled up to the top of the tree. If it had been a stronger-looking tree, I think I'd have followed him.

'OMIGOD!' whispered Tilly. 'Please say these people are on their way to a very elaborate fancy-dress party.'

'Would you believe me if I did?'

'I'd really want to,' she whispered.

But I knew this was no fancy-dress party. I'd been right all along – we had gone back in time.

Usually, being right is nice, but at that moment I very much wished that I had been wrong. This whole thing was starting to get a bit scary.

The chariot stopped and the three people jumped down. The boy held the horses' heads while the two men walked slowly towards us.

For a minute, the only sound was of the horses' stamping feet and the rattle of their harnesses.

One man pointed at our school uniforms and they both laughed. Then the other man spoke in a language I'd never heard before.

'I'm sorry,' said Tilly bravely. 'We don't speak . . . well, whatever language you're speaking, we don't speak it. You don't happen to speak English, do you?'

The men stared at her, then one man pointed at me.

'I think they want you to say something,' said Tilly.

'Er . . . my friend and I are a bit thirsty,' I said. 'Do you know if there's anywhere around here where we can get something to drink?'

Now the men said lots more stuff, but none of it made any sense to me.

Then one of them grabbed Tilly's schoolbag and threw it into the back of the chariot.

'Hey!' said Tilly. 'My schoolbooks are in there and, trust me, you wouldn't do that if you knew my teacher.'

The man didn't look like he was afraid of anything – not even our totally scary teacher. He said something else, and then he pointed at us and then pointed at the chariot. You didn't need to be a genius to understand what he was saying.

'What are we going to do? I really want to get my schoolbag back, but I'm so not going into that filthy chariot,' whispered Tilly.

'No offence, but our parents told us we should never take lifts from strangers,' I said loudly, trying to sound brave and polite at the same time.

The man slowly reached down and pulled a sword from its holder at his side. He pointed it in our direction.

I gulped. I knew we were in trouble – double trouble now that Tilly was with me.

Tilly grabbed my arm. 'Say something,' she said.

'Do you believe in time travel now?' I whispered.

Tilly had gone pale. 'Yes. I'm sorry, Lauren, for not believing you before. But I sooo believe you now.'

The man waved the sword in the air and it glinted dangerously in the bright sunlight.

'If we die here, do we just find ourselves back at home, like nothing happened?' whispered Tilly.

'I don't know,' I whispered back. 'Maybe if we die here, we're just . . . you know . . . dead.'

'I don't really want to find out the hard way, do you?'

I shook my head.

Then, holding hands, the two of us walked slowly towards the chariot.

3

Trust me, chariots really aren't a comfortable way to travel. The men and the boy stood at the front, while Tilly and I sat behind them, clinging on to the sides. At every bump in the road, I felt like we were both going to be flung out. (Which would have been fine except I'm fairly sure the men would have just picked us up and flung us straight back in again.)

I tried to figure out where and when we might be, but the constant bumping of the chariot made it impossible to think properly.

'Is Saturn still following us?' I asked, as soon as I dared to open my mouth.

'I haven't seen him for a while.'

I'd been afraid she was going to say that. At first, we'd seen Saturn trotting along the side of the road behind us, but he couldn't run very fast and he'd quickly fallen far behind.

'He's probably at home, trying to explain to my parents that he's managed to lose us forever,' I said.

'Don't say that,' Tilly replied, putting her arm round me. 'I bet he's hiding somewhere, waiting for an opportunity to rescue us.'

I huddled close to her and tried to believe that she was right.

In front, the two men were talking to each other.

'What language are they speaking?' asked Tilly.

'I don't know. All I know for sure is that it's not English and it's not French.'

'And it's not Spanish, because I'd recognize that after my holiday there last year.'

Then one of the men shook his fist at us and the other one reached for his sword, and Tilly and I figured it was time for us to be quiet.

After ages, we passed a few stone houses. The boy pulled hard on the reins and the chariot slowed down and then stopped completely. As soon as the bumpy motion ceased, I felt sick and dizzy.

I looked at Tilly and saw that she was pale and scared-looking. I held her hand and tried to look brave.

One of the men shouted something and a woman came out of a house.

'That woman looks kind of familiar,' I said to Tilly. 'Maybe Saturn has brought us to meet some of my ancestors.'

Tilly shook her head. 'I doubt if that woman is your ancestor. She just looks familiar because there's a picture of a woman exactly like her in our history book.'

'In which chapter?' I asked, half afraid of the answer.

'In the chapter on –'

'– Ancient Rome,' I suddenly remembered and finished the sentence for her.

At last, the chariot and the clothes the men were wearing started to make sense.

'So the men are speaking Latin,' said Tilly. 'That's why it sounded so strange.'

'Saturn has brought us to Ancient Rome,' I whispered. 'I can't believe it.'

'I can't believe it either – but it's true . . . isn't it?'

I nodded slowly. 'It looks like it.'

The last time I'd time-travelled, I'd stayed in the same country, and had gone back less than a hundred years. Now I was far, far away from home – and even with Tilly beside me, it was totally scary. Suddenly I wished that I was safe with my family, with nothing more serious than a history project to worry about.

The men said something to the woman and she went back into the house. When she came back a minute later she was carrying a large bowl of water. She handed the bowl to the men, who took turns to drink.

As I watched, I forgot all about being scared. I forgot all about Ancient Rome and chariots and scary, glinting swords. My mouth felt drier than it ever had before. I felt like my tongue was stuck to the roof of my mouth. Beside me, Tilly was trying to moisten her dry and cracked lips. One man passed the bowl towards the boy, laughing as some of the precious water sloshed over the edge. As the boy held it to his lips, he looked up and his huge dark brown eyes met mine. Without taking any water, he passed the bowl to me. I drank greedily and quickly passed the bowl to Tilly. She drank all but the last few drops, which she passed back to the boy.

'Sorry,' she said, as he drank. 'You see we haven't had a drop of water for thousands of years.'

The boy smiled at her, almost like he could understand. Then the woman took her bowl back and we continued our journey.

4

We passed more and more houses, and soon we were in the middle of a city.

'This must be Rome,' sighed Tilly. 'I've always wanted to visit Rome.'

'Me too, but given a choice, I'd skip the whole chariot and sword and scary-men thing. I'd kind of prefer to be here in our real time. I'd like to be travelling by air-conditioned bus and staying in a nice hotel, with a leisure centre and a pizza restaurant.'

Tilly laughed, and for one small second as I laughed with her, I managed to forget how scared I was.

Just then we pulled up next to a huge wooden gate. The men jumped down from the chariot and waved at us to follow them. The boy gave us a sympathetic look. It didn't make me feel better. Did he know something we didn't?

I looked all around, hoping to see Saturn, but there was no sign of him. Had we lost him forever?

Tilly grabbed her schoolbag and we jumped down from the chariot. The firm ground under my feet felt strange. The two men were talking to another man.

'Maybe we should make a run for it while they're distracted?' I whispered.

Tilly shook her head. 'Haven't you seen those swords? They don't look like they're used for decoration. I wish I had a gun in my schoolbag.'

'I thought you were a pacifist.'

'I am, but this is an emergency. And if I had a gun, I wouldn't use it. I'd just threaten them with it.'

'Anyway, these people have never seen guns,' I said. 'They wouldn't know to be afraid.'

'That's true,' said Tilly, rooting through her schoolbag. 'I wonder if they'd be afraid of this cheese sandwich I forgot to eat at lunchtime?'

The sight of the sandwich reminded me of something.

'I'm starving,' I said.

Tilly, who is always really generous, carefully tore the sandwich in two, and we started to eat.

It was totally weird. There we were in Ancient Rome, eating the food that Tilly had prepared that morning in her nice, safe kitchen, back when we were living our real lives. How could things change so much, so quickly?

Just as we were wiping the last crumbs from our mouths, one of the men stepped forward and took Tilly by the arm. He led her inside the building, and far too afraid to be left on my own, I followed.

We were in a huge open area, a bit like a market place. People were pushing and shoving. The man led us to a small platform and indicated that we should climb up.

'Maybe we're going to be in a play,' I said hopefully as I went up the steps. 'Or this could be the Roman version of *The X Factor*. Have you got your tin whistle in your bag?'

'I doubt if it's *The X Factor*,' said Tilly. 'Even

Simon Cowell couldn't get away with treating the contestants like this.'

The man climbed on to the platform beside us and began to shout out something. Gradually people began to walk over, and soon a crowd had gathered. The man suddenly seemed nice and friendly, patting our hair and smiling at us.

'Maybe things aren't so bad,' said Tilly. 'This could be where they bring people who are lost, so their relatives can find them – sort of like customer services in the supermarket. Pity he doesn't know that none of our relatives is going to be born for thousands of years. No one's showing up to claim us any time soon.'

Suddenly I could feel the blood draining from my face.

'Tilly,' I whispered. 'I've just remembered something important about Roman times.'

'What?'

I could hardly get the words out. 'In Roman times . . . they had . . . slaves.'

'OMIGOD!' she gasped. 'This guy isn't trying to reunite us with our families. He's trying to sell us.'

The man was still talking. He pointed at our crumpled uniforms and the crowd laughed.

Tilly put her arm round me. 'OK, so we don't like wearing these ugly uniforms either,' she muttered. 'But it's a school rule. We don't get a choice in the matter.'

I knew she was trying to make me feel better, but it didn't help. I was too scared.

And where was Saturn? Why wasn't he here to save us?

A few people stepped forward and stared extra closely at us. One woman climbed on to the platform. She looked inside my ears, and then she took Tilly's hands and examined her fingernails. Tilly grabbed her hands back and the crowd laughed again.

Just then the crowd went silent as a huge, tall man pushed his way to the front. He was dark-skinned and hairy, and on one of his arms, a huge deep scar ran all the way from his wrist to his shoulder. He was the most evil-looking man I had ever seen.

'That man looks a bit like the ogre in the pantomime we went to last Christmas,' said Tilly.

'Maybe,' I replied. 'But in the pantomime, he was scary and funny at the same time. This guy seems to be concentrating on the scary part.'

The ogre looked closely at Tilly and me, and then he spoke to the man on the platform.

Tilly held my hand.

'It's going to be OK, Lauren,' she said. 'It's going to be OK.'

If it was going to be OK, then why was Tilly shaking so badly? And why was she squeezing my hand like she was trying to grind every one of my bones to a fine powder?

After a long, heated discussion, the evil-looking ogre loosened a leather pouch that hung from his belt. He pulled two coins from it and handed them to the first man. Then they shook hands and the first man walked away. The ogre said something unintelligible to Tilly and me, and then he took each of us by the arm and led us from the market place.

 5

A short while later, we were walking along a
dusty road, with Tilly and me in front and
the ogre a few paces behind. Every time I glanced
back, the ogre growled something, so I decided it
was best to keep my eyes on the track ahead.

Tilly and I whispered together to try to make
ourselves feel better, but it wasn't easy. When you've
just discovered that you are hundreds of kilometres
and thousands of years away from home, it's bad
enough.

When you've also found yourself sold as a slave to
the most evil-looking man you've ever seen, then
chatting about pop stars and TV programmes is
never going to be much of a distraction.

'I'm going to throw away a few books,' said Tilly after a while. 'My schoolbag is too heavy and my shoulders are killing me.'

'No!' I protested. 'Don't do that. This is the past, remember? All of the stuff in your bag could be useful at some stage. What you have in that bag is all we have to keep us going while we're here. It's not like you can just pop home later on if there's something else you want.'

'Am I likely to want my history book? I don't need to read about Roman times. I can just open my eyes and see it all around me, can't I?'

I tried another approach. 'Your dad will kill you if you go home without some of your books.'

'You're right, but I wouldn't care. You have no idea how much I'd like to be at home now, with my dad shouting at me over a stupid lost schoolbook. I thought you said time-travelling was fun?'

'Well, last time it was – sort of – when it wasn't totally, totally scary.'

Tilly sighed. 'Maybe I wasn't listening properly when you mentioned that part.'

'Here,' I said, feeling sorry for her. 'Let me carry your bag for a while, so you can have a bit of a rest.'

'Thanks, Lauren,' she said as she passed her bag to me. Then we walked on in silence.

'We've got to get away from this man,' said Tilly after a while. 'There's still no sign of Saturn, so it's up to us to help ourselves.'

'But –'

'We have to,' she insisted. 'The ogre's paid money for us, remember. That means we're valuable to him. As soon as we get to wherever we're going, he'll probably lock us up in a dungeon and we'll never get away. It's now or never.'

I still wasn't convinced. 'But he's much bigger and taller than us. If we run away, he'll easily catch us.'

'If we run in different directions, he can't catch us both.'

I so didn't like the sound of this.

Tilly continued. 'Don't you see, Lauren? It's the only way. Even if he catches one of us, the other one will be free to come up with a rescue plan.'

I still didn't like the sound of it.

'But you've seen his sword. What if he kills the person he catches?'

Tilly shook her head. 'He won't. We're worth money to him, remember? He might be really angry, but he won't hurt us. Trust me, Lauren, we have to do this.'

Tilly is very clever and logical, and I usually do trust her, but now . . . I wasn't so sure. What she was suggesting was so totally scary, I couldn't even think about it properly. But I was too tired and frightened to argue any more, so I just listened while Tilly explained her plan.

'What we do is this: we wait until we get to a place where there's some cover. I'll give the signal and then we each run in different directions. The ogre can only run after one of us, so the other one will hide. Then, when he gives up looking, he'll keep going to wherever he's going, and the free person can follow.'

'And then what?'

'And then the free person will rescue the captive.'

'How?'

Tilly hesitated.

'I haven't got to that bit of the plan yet. Whoever it is will have to figure it out when the time comes.'

At home, Tilly and I often play Would You Rather?, but it's usually stupid stuff like, Would You Rather have a boy's haircut for a year or dress up as a giraffe for a year? I never, ever thought I'd have to decide whether I'd rather be a slave belonging to the most evil-looking man in the world, or lost in Roman times trying to free a slave belonging to the most evil-looking man in the world.

And so we walked on. Part of me hoped that we would never come to a suitable place for escape. It was the straightest road I'd ever walked on, and all around us there were just flat fields stretching away as far as I could see. After a while, though, we saw in the distance that there were woods on both sides of the road.

'Yesss,' said Tilly softly.

'Nooo,' I said to myself.

Tilly took my hand and squeezed it. 'We have to be brave, Lauren,' she whispered. 'If we're brave, everything will turn out right in the end.'

Who says?

Before long we got to the wooded area, and Tilly had issued her final instruction. 'We'll distract the ogre and then, on my signal, we'll both run as fast as we can. I'll run left and you run right. OK?'

I nodded. Tilly squeezed my hand one more time. 'Love you, Lauren,' she said.

'Love you, Tilly,' I said in a weird, croaky kind of voice.

Then really quickly, she turned and shouted at the ogre. 'Hey, what's that behind you?' she called, pointing to the sky above his left shoulder.

Of course he couldn't understand the words, but Tilly's pointing finger was clear enough. The ogre stopped walking and looked behind him.

'Now!' Tilly whispered. 'Run!'

I hesitated for a second, half afraid that she wasn't going to run, but then she was gone, darting through the first trees on the left-hand side of the road.

Every instinct urged me to follow her, but somehow I resisted and began to run to my right.

Tilly is my very best friend in the whole world, but as I ran, the same words kept racing through my head – *Please make him go after Tilly. Please make him go after Tilly.* (I know that makes me sound like a horrible person, but I was so totally terrified I couldn't get those bad, selfish thoughts out of my head.)

My heart was pounding so fast, I thought it was going to leap right out of my chest. And soon, even though I didn't dare to look back, the sound of crashing feet made it very clear that my wish wasn't going to come true. The ogre was coming after me, and he was getting closer.

I ran like I had never run before. I ran like an Olympic medallist who'd been training for four long years. I ran even though twigs were flying into my face and scraping my skin. I ran even though my legs were aching and I was gasping for breath.

But it wasn't enough.

Before I'd gone any distance at all, I could feel the ogre's hand grabbing Tilly's rucksack, which I still had on my back. Desperately, I tried to wriggle free of the straps, but it was too late. The ogre used his other hand to grab my arm. I pulled and kicked and screamed, but he didn't let go.

He shouted at me in Latin, and I prayed that Tilly's prediction of him not hurting us would turn out to be right.

Then, when I couldn't scream or kick any more, the ogre pulled me back to where we had last seen Tilly. Just as we reached that point, I saw one of Tilly's feet disappearing into the branches of a huge tree not too far from the side of the road. Clearly the ogre hadn't seen her, though, as he began to march through the trees, shouting and dragging me as he went.

We trailed backwards and forwards for ages. Once or twice we passed really close to the tree where Tilly was hiding, but I didn't dare betray her by looking up. (Even though part of me sort of hoped that she'd jump down and surrender, as I was totally afraid without her.)

Eventually, the ogre gave up. He dragged me towards the road, and pushed me forward. I barely had the strength to walk by then, so running away was completely out of the question. I numbly put one foot in front of the other, never daring to look back, but always hoping that somewhere behind me Tilly was following, and that she had a plan.

 6

When it felt like I had walked a hundred
kilometres, it started to get dark. I was
feeling even more scared than before, when we
came to a huge farm. The ogre pushed me through
the gates in the direction of a man standing outside
a long, low building. The ogre walked towards the
man and they talked for a long time. The ogre
pointed at me and then pointed back along the
road. I guessed he was telling the story of Tilly's
escape and I hoped they wouldn't consider it worth
their while to go looking for her.

After a while, the ogre pushed me towards the
building. I saw that the door was held closed by a big
plank of wood that slotted into two pieces of metal on

either side of the door frame. The ogre raised the plank of wood, opened the door and shoved me inside. Behind me, I could hear the thud of the wooden plank falling into place once more. For the first time, I felt a glimmer of hope. If Tilly was somewhere nearby, maybe she could come and open the door and release me as soon as the two men went away.

I turned to face the room. Many pairs of eyes were staring at me. It was like the first day in a new school – only a million times worse. There were maybe twenty women and girls in the room, ranging from children who looked a lot younger than me, right up to women old enough to be my mother. Some of the younger girls giggled. The ones my age looked bored, and the older women looked at me with some sympathy.

One of the older women came over to me. Her face was thin and wrinkled, but she looked kind. She said something to me in Latin.

'Sorry,' I said. 'I can't understand.'

She smiled and said something in what sounded like a different language.

I shook my head. 'Sorry,' I said again.

She patted my arm and then pointed at herself and said 'Marca.'

That was clear enough for me. I pointed to myself and said 'Lauren.'

The woman put her hand over her mouth and laughed.

'Lau-ren,' she said.

I nodded and smiled. I really didn't want to be hanging out here for long, but while I was, I figured it was no harm to have a friend or two.

Marca took my arm. I tried not to wince as she put her hand on the part that was still sore from when the ogre had pulled me through the wood. She led me to a line of low, narrow beds at the back of the room. Most had a few belongings on them, but one was bare except for two small, light blankets. Marca pointed at it. I wondered if I should lie down, then I figured that was a bit stupid as no one else was in bed. So I pulled Tilly's schoolbag off my shoulders and put it on the bed. That must have been the right thing to do because

Marca smiled and led me to the centre of the room. She sat on a bench next to a table and began to talk to the woman next to her.

I sat down and looked around properly. Everyone was dressed much the same, in greyish, knee-length tunics, so I felt a bit stupid in my royal blue school uniform. On their feet, everyone was wearing leather sandals that wouldn't have looked out of place in the window of our local shoe shop.

It was totally weird. All these women had to be slaves, but they didn't seem to mind very much. There were no chains, and no one was crying or moaning or trying to escape. Everyone was just getting on with stuff. Some were sewing, some were fixing their hair and some were sitting on the floor playing a game with stones. A group of girls my age were standing in a corner chatting. They could have been hanging out at the end of my road at home – I half expected one of them to pull a phone out from under their tunics and start texting.

Then a door at the back of the room opened and two women came out carrying huge trays of food. I thought there might be a stampede, but everyone very politely and quietly came to sit at the table. The trays were passed round and everyone took some food. Marca turned to me and smiled. She took a piece of bread from the tray and handed it to me.

'*Panis*,' she said.

'*Panis*,' I repeated, and she smiled.

The she reached out and took a boiled egg from the tray.

'*Eggus?*' I said, making everyone at the table laugh.

Marca handed me the egg. '*Ovo*,' she said.

I repeated the word after her and she smiled again. I like learning new words, but I so didn't want to be hanging around long enough to actually need them.

I ate the egg and the bread, and drank some sweet juice from a wooden cup.

After the food was cleared away, Marca talked to the other women and I took the opportunity to check out the room properly.

It was long and narrow. Apart from the door I'd come in, there were only two other doors in the whole place. I looked through one and saw a small kitchen area, where some women were rinsing out cups and tidying away the leftover food.

The other door was half open and I peeped through. It was dark, and at first I couldn't see much. A few women were sitting on a bench that ran round three sides of the wall. They were chatting and laughing. I wondered why they had chosen to hang out in such a smelly room. Then, as my eyes got used to the dark, I realized that the bench had holes cut in it. While I was trying to take this in, two more slaves came in and, taking no notice of me, began to pull up their tunics. One waved at me and pointed at the empty hole next to her. Suddenly I understood. I shook my head and backed away quickly, hoping that Tilly would rescue me before I needed to go to the toilet.

There were a number of openings in the wall of the main room – windows without glass. They were too narrow for me to fit through, but just in case

45

someone extremely skinny showed up, there was also a big metal bar across the centre of each.

Clearly there was only one way out of this room, and it was blocked by the heavy plank of wood.

The situation would have been completely hopeless – if I didn't have a clever, brave friend on the outside, just waiting for her chance to whisk me away to freedom.

7

I was curled up on my narrow slave's bed, sleeping
soundly. In my dream, I could hear Tilly calling
my name. In my dream, I could feel someone
pulling my hair. I sat up, suddenly fully awake.

'At last! I thought I was going to have to set your
bed on fire to wake you up.'

I turned to see Tilly peeping through the narrow
window behind me. I looked around. All the other
slaves were asleep. I jumped out of bed and did my
best to hug Tilly through the tiny, barred window.
Even though we were separated by a thick stone wall,
just knowing that she was there made me feel better.

'Have you seen Saturn?' I asked as I finally pulled
away from the awkward hug.

She shook her head. 'I've looked and called, but there's no sign of him.'

The thought of Saturn being lost was very scary, and the thought of Tilly and me being stuck in Ancient Rome without him was even scarier. I knew I had to change the subject.

'You were right, Tilly,' I said. 'Splitting up was a great idea. And I've figured out a plan for you to rescue me. All you have to do is lift up the wooden bar on the outside of that door over there.'

I was helpfully pointing towards the door, but to my surprise, Tilly didn't rush over to open it.

'So what are you waiting for?' I asked.

She sighed. 'I'm waiting for you to tell me which part of your plan explains what I should do about the huge man and the two wolf-like dogs that are sitting outside that door.'

I groaned. Maybe my mum is right. She always says that if something seems too good to be true, then it probably is. But there was no way I was giving up that easily.

'Maybe you could poison the man and the dogs,' I suggested.

'With the vial of poison that I have conveniently tucked into my uniform pocket?'

'Very funny. Not!' I said. 'Have you any other bright ideas?'

She shook her head. 'Sorry. Maybe we should wait until tomorrow. Maybe you'll be let out for a walk or something, and you could run away.'

'I'm a slave,' I said. 'I don't think I'll be given a whole lot of time for going on a nice walk or a little trip into town for a spot of window-shopping.'

But I knew she was right. We were both tired and scared. Surely things would be better in the morning?

'Fine,' I said. 'Let's wait until tomorrow.' I hesitated and then continued. 'I'm a slave – it's kind of a new experience. What do you think tomorrow is going to be like for me?'

'I don't know. But I peeped in earlier and none of the other slaves looks too unhappy, so maybe it's not so bad.'

'Maybe,' I said, not really convinced.

'And they gave you lots of food.'

I suddenly had a horrible thought. 'You don't think it's like the evil witch in *Hansel and Gretel*? You don't think they're fattening us up so they can eat us?'

'Nah. The history book never said anything about cannibals in Roman times. You'll be fine.'

'You're sure?'

'Sure I'm sure,' she said, and I believed her because I so very much wanted to.

'Lauren,' she said suddenly.

'What?'

'That bed looks really comfy.'

I shrugged. 'It's not so bad.'

'And Lauren?'

'What?'

'I'm starving.'

Suddenly I realized that our history book was right when it said that being a slave in Roman times wasn't always the worst thing that could happen to you. At least I had a bed and food.

Then I remembered the kitchen.

'Hang on,' I said.

I wasn't really sure if I was allowed into the kitchen, but there was only one way to find out. I tiptoed across the room and into the kitchen. I grabbed a piece of bread from a table. In a cupboard I found a big jug of water and I poured some into a wooden cup. Then I returned to Tilly with my treasures.

Poor Tilly, whose manners are usually so perfect, grabbed the bread and shoved it into her mouth. Then she threw back her head and drank every drop of water.

'Thanks,' she said, handing me the cup.

'So what's the plan?' I said.

She sighed. 'I'm going to find a ditch or somewhere to sleep, while you snuggle up in your cosy bed.'

I turned and picked up one of my thin blankets. 'Here,' I said. 'This might make you a bit more comfy.'

Tilly took the blanket and wrapped it round her

51

shoulders. Then she turned and looked into the darkness. 'Do you think there were wolves in Roman times?' she asked.

'Yeah, of course there were – remember Romulus and Remus?'

Tilly gasped and I tried to reassure her.

'The wolves took care of Romulus and Remus,' I said. 'So maybe they'll do the same for you.'

'Thanks,' said Tilly. 'Call me fussy if you like, but I don't really fancy setting up home with a pack of wolves.'

I giggled. 'I'm sure it won't come to that. Don't worry, Tilly. You'll be fine out there, and I'll be fine in here.'

'We'll all be fine,' said Tilly, sounding like she didn't believe a word of what she was saying.

Then we held hands for a second before she vanished into the night.

 8

I was dreaming that I was at home making popcorn, when I woke to feel someone shaking my feet.

'Go away, Mum,' I mumbled. 'It's Saturday. Let me sleep.'

Then I heard a voice and I knew that unless she'd spent the whole night at Latin school, it couldn't be my mum. I sat up and rubbed my eyes.

Marca was standing at the end of my bed, smiling. She pointed to the table, where most of the slaves were already eating. I followed Marca to the table, and she handed me a steaming bowl.

Great . . . porridge. My favourite . . . not.

I wondered if they had any cornflakes or Coco

Pops. I wondered what the Latin for Rice Krispies might be.

I took a small taste of the food and then edged the bowl away. Marca saw me and pushed the bowl closer again, miming eating it. I looked around and saw that everyone was devouring their food. Either they loved porridge, or they knew they weren't getting anything else anytime soon.

Marca reached for a jug and poured some honey over my porridge, using my wooden spoon to stir it in.

I tried some and it didn't taste too bad, so I copied everyone else and ate until my bowl was empty.

Shortly afterwards, the big door opened and the ogre and three other men walked into the room. All the slaves lined up and, not wanting to draw attention to myself, I joined them.

The ogre led the way to an open area, where we were divided into groups. (It so wasn't like the first day in a new school. There was no welcome talk or anything. I was just shoved into one of the groups, and expected to get on with it.)

My group was taken to a field full of onions. One of the men handed me a bag made of strong canvas. I copied everyone else and slung the bag over my shoulder. Then I did as they did, walking along the rows of onions, picking as I went and piling the bulbs into my bag. At the end of each row, I emptied them into a big, wheeled cart. All the time, two huge men with swords stood watching our every move and spoiling any hopes I had of sneaking away to look for Tilly.

I thought of my last time-travel trip, when I'd met Mikey, who was working in his carrot field, and I wondered if all time travel involved boring farm stuff.

Soon, though, I was too tired to think of anything. My arms were getting sunburned, my feet felt like they were on fire and I thought my back was going to break.

After ages, some of the younger slaves came along with jugs of water, and I drank like it was the sweetest thing I had ever tasted. Then, before I had time to lick my lips, the men were shouting at us to continue with our work.

When it felt like I had picked enough onions to keep our local supermarket going for weeks, one of the men shouted something and all of the workers walked to the cart, where they took off their bags and lined up.

We were led back to our house, but instead of going inside, everyone sat in the shade of some trees outside. I looked all around, hoping to see Tilly peeping over a wall or something, but there was no sign of her. I scanned the trees hoping to see Saturn, but there was no sign of him either. It probably didn't matter anyway, as we were being watched by the ogre and four armed men, and I knew there was zero chance of escaping.

Some women brought out trays of food and everyone dived in. There was more bread, and cheese and grapes – it was a bit like the stuff my mum serves at the end of the meal when she's having a very fancy dinner party.

At the thought of my mum, I could feel tears come to my eyes. What would she say if she could see me sitting in the sunshine without sunscreen on?

What would she say if she could see me working as a slave, picking onions while being guarded by men armed with scary-looking swords?

After the food was gone, Marca came over to me. She looked shocked when she saw my red arms and face. She went into the house and came out holding a bowl of some kind of ointment. She made me hold out my arms and she rubbed the ointment on to them with gentle strokes of her long fingers. Then she put ointment on my face, carefully rubbing it on to my cheeks and ears. Suddenly her kindness was too much for me, and I started to sob. Marca put down the bowl and hugged me and stroked my hair. As she did so, she kept murmuring the same thing over and over. I wondered what she was saying. Probably something like 'Don't worry, the first ten years of being a slave are the hardest,' which so wasn't a consolation to me.

After a while, I was too tired to cry any more. I looked around and saw that most of the slaves were lying down on the dusty ground. That seemed like a good idea to me, so I pulled away from Marca and tried to find a comfortable patch of bare earth on which to lay my head. Marca patted my arm for a minute, and soon I could feel her lying down beside me. Then I fell into a deep and dreamless sleep.

9

When I awoke, I knew exactly where I was and I so wasn't happy to be there. I sat up and rubbed my eyes, wondering how soon it would be before we'd have to go back to work. I didn't have to wonder about that for too long, though, as the ogre shouted something and all the slaves began to stand up, dusting down their tunics and stretching their legs.

Then I noticed that everyone was staring at the track leading towards the gate. Two people were walking along it. One was an elegant-looking man, dressed in a toga. He had grey, wavy hair and he moved like he was someone important – like he was used to being stared at. Beside him was a girl who looked about my age. Like the slaves, she was wearing a knee-length tunic – but there the similarity ended. The slaves' tunics were heavy and rough-looking, but I could see that the girl's tunic was made of fine, delicate fabric and was trimmed at the hem with gold and silver threads. Round her shoulders she had a pale blue shawl.

The slaves were pointing and whispering among themselves, and at first I was really sorry that I couldn't understand what they were saying. Were we looking at two Ancient Roman celebrities? Should I be impressed? Should I be asking for their autographs?

Then I realized that I really didn't care who these people were. All I knew was that, while they were there, I might get a few minutes' break from picking onions.

The strangers were next to us now. The girl stared right at me – a bit rudely, I thought – and the man spoke to the ogre, who didn't seem so confident any more, half bowing and speaking in a whiny voice. Then the man in the toga surveyed the group of slaves and pointed at me. I could feel my sunburned face go even redder as everyone else stared at me too.

The ogre and the elegant-looking man talked for a long time. Then the ogre laughed and held up four fingers. The man shook his head and held up two fingers. I knew exactly what was going on. Not only were they talking about me like I wasn't standing right there, they were also haggling over how much I was worth. Finally, both men held up three fingers. It looked like the deal was done.

The man pulled a small leather pouch from the folds of his toga, took out three coins and handed them to the ogre. Then the man and the girl began to walk back towards the gate.

I stood there, unsure of what to do next.

Was I supposed to follow these strangers? If I did follow them, was everyone going to laugh and pull me back and hand me my onion sack for another few hours of hard work?

Before I could make up my mind, Marca raced inside and returned with Tilly's schoolbag over her shoulder. She handed me the bag, then smiled and patted my arm in a vague kind of way. Then she gave me a gentle push and I knew what I had to do.

I gave her a quick hug, then followed my new owners and set off for the next stage of my journey. I had no idea where I was going, but I sooo hoped it wasn't going to involve another onion farm.

When I got to the gate, I turned round for a last look. Already the slaves were on their way back to work and no one was looking at me. I wondered how many times you have to watch people being bought and sold before it becomes almost normal.

Neither the man nor the girl spoke while we walked through the gate and on to the road. I couldn't have answered them anyway, but the silence was making me kind of nervous. Then, under the shade of a tall tree, I saw a big wooden vehicle. It looked like some kind of ancient caravan. In front were two huge white horses that were being held by a young boy who was dressed like a slave. The girl walked up to the caravan and pulled open a door. She stepped inside and beckoned to me to follow her.

I hesitated. I sooo wanted to get far away from the ogre and the onion farm, but what if that meant getting far away from Tilly and Saturn too?

I looked around desperately, hoping to see Tilly sitting on a wall, or Saturn lazing on the low branch of a tree, but there was no sign of either of them.

Inside the caravan, I could hear the girl's voice, and then I heard the wonderful sound of familiar laughter and a voice I knew almost as well as my own.

'Are you coming up here or do I have to drag you?'

I scrambled up the steps and into the caravan and threw myself into Tilly's arms.

'What happened?' I said. 'What are you doing here? What am *I* doing here? Who are these people? Have you seen Saturn?'

Tilly shook her head. 'Sorry. I haven't seen Saturn at all. But let me introduce my new friend. Prima, this is Lauren; Lauren, this is Prima.'

I didn't know what the formal greeting in Roman times was, so I sort of waved at Prima and she smiled at me and sort of waved back.

Then the door opened and the man looked inside. He seemed happy to see that we were smiling and trying to communicate.

'*Pater*,' said Prima, pointing at the man.

'Bet you any money that means father,' said Tilly.

Then Prima pointed at him again. '*Julius*,' she said.

Tilly's mouth opened wide. 'OMG. I don't believe it,' she said. 'Don't tell me we've just ended up with Julius Caesar? How amazingly cool would that be? Do you think we should bow or curtsey or something?'

I was too stunned to answer any of Tilly's questions. All I could do was stare at the man and gasp, 'Julius Caesar.'

Prima and her father were laughing like this was the funniest thing they had ever heard. Eventually, the man wiped his eyes and pointed to his chest. '*Titus Julius Arcanus*,' he said.

'*Julius Caesar mortuus est . . .*' said Prima.

'Like post-mortem,' I said to Tilly. 'Julius Caesar must be dead already. That'll help us to figure out exactly when we are.'

'Well, it would if we knew when exactly Julius Caesar lived and died.'

She was right, but I realized that I didn't really care what the date was. All I wanted to do was find Saturn and then get very, very far away from the ogre.

Julius spoke to Prima and closed the caravan door. A few seconds later, the caravan began to move, and through an opening I could see Julius walking behind us.

Prima, Tilly and I sat on the cushion-lined benches that ran all round the inside of the caravan. I was so happy I could hardly speak. Prima and her father seemed like kind people, and Tilly and I were back together.

'So tell me,' I said to Tilly, 'what's been going on.'

Tilly took a deep breath and began to explain. 'Well, it all started kind of badly. Last night I slept in a shed thing with no door, and it sooo wasn't fun. I was cold and afraid, and I had no idea how I was going to rescue you. And then this morning, I was watching when you came out into the field with the

65

other slaves and began to work. And I felt so sorry for you, and so sorry for myself too. And then I saw all the guards with swords and I knew there was no way I was going to be able to help you escape, and I couldn't find Saturn anywhere and . . .'

She stopped talking, and I could see tears coming to her eyes.

'And?' I prompted her gently.

'And that's when I made up my mind. I decided I was going to look for the ogre and give myself up.'

I gasped. 'But your original idea was a great one. I was totally scared, but I knew we'd done the right thing. If you'd given yourself up, we'd never have escaped. We'd both have been slaves forever.'

Tilly nodded. 'I know. But I couldn't think of anything else to do. Before long, I was probably going to starve to death, or get eaten by wolves or something, and then I couldn't rescue you anyway. So you'd still be a slave forever and I'd be dead, and that sooo wasn't the way I wanted all this to work out. And . . .' Her voice trailed off.

'And what . . .? I prompted her again.

Her voice was almost a whisper. 'And without you, Lauren, I was so lonely and so afraid, I thought I was going to die.'

'And then what happened?'

'Well, as I was walking up to the gate of the farm, I felt sooo bad. It was all much, much too scary for me. I sat down by the side of the road and cried and cried for ages. I was crying so much I didn't even hear the caravan coming along, and next thing I knew, Prima and her father were standing next to me and talking to me, and they looked nice, so I just smiled and pretended I had the first notion of what they were on about. And after a while, Julius nodded and Prima hugged him.'

'And then?'

'And then I realized that I was starving because I hadn't eaten since you gave me that bread last night. So I rubbed my stomach, and I felt totally stupid, but Prima understood straight away. She got a basket from the caravan and gave me bread and fruit and cheese.'

'That's what I had for lunch too,' I said. 'The cheese wasn't that nice though. It . . .'

I noticed that Tilly was looking at me with raised eyebrows and knew that she wanted to get on with her story.

'Oops, sorry,' I said, and she continued.

'Then Prima tried to get me to go into the caravan. I knew I'd be safe with her, but I couldn't just go away and leave you. I looked over the wall and saw that you and all the other slaves were asleep. So I kept pointing to you and trying to explain that I wanted you to come too, but Prima and Julius didn't understand, and there were so many slaves there, they probably didn't even know which one I was pointing at. And then, for the first time in my life, I realized I was glad to be wearing my school uniform. I pointed at it, and I tried to make Prima and Julius see that I wanted them to get the other girl who was wearing the same uniform, and I got down on my knees and begged.'

'Really? You did that for me?'

She nodded. 'I had to. I had to make them see

how important it was. And then they seemed to understand and they tried to make me go with them, but now that there seemed to be another way, I sooo wasn't going to risk getting caught by the ogre. So they went into the farm without me.'

'And you hid in the caravan?'

She nodded again. 'And I so hoped that Prima and Julius had understood properly, and that they weren't going to show up with an ancient old granny instead of you. And then you came and now . . . everything's perfect . . . except that we don't know where Saturn is . . . and –'

I finished the sentence for her.

'– and without Saturn, we have no way of getting back home again.'

Suddenly the joy of being back with Tilly began to fade. Prima and Julius seemed nice, but without Saturn, Tilly and I were still in a lot of trouble.

I wished I'd paid more attention in history class.

'Do you know anything about the Romans and cats?' I said to Tilly. 'Did they eat them or worship them or what?'

Tilly shrugged. 'Neither, as far as I know. I think they just had them as pets, like we do. Anyway, Saturn can find his way through hundreds and thousands of years. I'm sure he'll be able to track us down. Don't worry, Lauren, it'll all turn out well in the end.'

She put her arm round me and for the first time in ages, I felt safe and happy.

The caravan trundled on for a while. Prima sat on the bench across from Tilly and me and smiled at us a lot. She didn't seem to mind that she couldn't talk to us. Every now and then, Tilly and I said something to each other, but we were both tired after our eventful day and soon we both lay back on the cushions and drifted off to sleep.

Suddenly, I woke up, aware that the caravan had stopped moving. I peeped out through the side window, but it didn't look like we'd arrived anywhere in particular. All I could see were fields. Beside me, Tilly sat up and rubbed her eyes.

Just at that moment I had a horrible thought.

'Oh no,' I whispered. 'Maybe Julius has changed

his mind about buying me. Maybe he wants to take me back. Maybe he's kept the receipt and can get a refund within thirty days.'

Tilly giggled. 'Don't be so paranoid, Lauren. Maybe we're stopping for a picnic or something.'

Prima stood up and opened the door of the caravan. She stepped outside, and came back seconds later, looking surprised.

'*Cattus*,' she said.

Tilly and I looked at each other and beamed. Even though we'd never studied Latin, it didn't take a genius to figure out what *cattus* meant. I jumped up from my seat and ran down the steps.

There, right in the middle of the road, was Saturn. He was licking his lips and almost smiling, like he was glad to see me. I raced over and picked him up and hugged him. Then Tilly caught up and the two of us stroked and petted him, as if he was the most wonderful thing we had ever seen.

Julius and Prima were smiling, and they didn't protest when Tilly and I climbed back into the caravan bringing Saturn with us.

As the caravan started to move again I caught Prima's eye. I pointed at Saturn. 'Saturn,' I said. 'My cat . . . I mean . . . *cattus.*'

To my surprise, Prima didn't smile and repeat the name. She looked very shocked, like I'd said something really bad.

'Saturn,' I said again and now Prima looked almost afraid.

'I don't think she likes your cat's name,' said Tilly.

'Clever of you to notice,' I said. 'Maybe she knows someone horrible who's called Saturn and that's why she doesn't like it.'

When I said the word again, Prima flinched and shook her head. I had no idea what was going on, but I figured it best not to do or say anything else that might upset her. She was all that stood between me and a long, hard life as an onion-picking slave.

'Sattie,' I said, and was pleased to see Prima smile.

She came over and stroked Saturn's head. 'Sattie,' she said slowly.

Then we all settled down and our journey continued.

10

Much, much later, the caravan slowed down
again. I looked out through an opening
and saw that we had turned off the road and
were going along a wide driveway. In the
distance, I could see a huge city with a mountain
behind it.

'OMG,' I said. 'There's the city we were in before
with the ogre. That has to be Rome.'

'How do you know?' asked Tilly.

'Well, it looks like Rome,' I said.

'And you've been to Rome how many times
exactly?' asked Tilly.

'Er . . . none. But there's a big hill over there, and
remember Romulus and Remus built Rome on a

hill. And look over there on the left – I think I can see the colosseum.'

Tilly looked where I was pointing. 'Oh, Lauren,' she said. ' I think you're right –we're in Ancient Rome and we're going to have so much fun. Let's not be scared any more. Time travel is totally amazing.'

She jumped up and we hugged for a long time.

I felt sorry for Prima, who was watching us and clearly not understanding what was going on.

'Rome?' I said to her, pointing at the city.

She looked puzzled for a minute and then smiled. '*Roma?*' she asked.

I nodded. 'Yes, *Roma*. That's it over there, isn't it?'

Prima laughed and shook her head.

I pointed to the city again and made my best questioning face at Prima. She seemed to understand.

'*Campania*,' she said.

'Never heard of it,' said Tilly. 'I so wish it was Rome. Hanging out in the colosseum would have been totally cool.'

I was disappointed too, but tried not to show it.

'Who cares if it's Rome or not?' I said. 'It's a city and I don't see a single onion farm.'

Tilly patted my arm. 'It's time to move on, Lauren,' she said. 'It's time to leave your onion-picking days behind you.'

I knew she was right. I'd only been a farm slave for a single day and it was probably time to stop whingeing about it.

Before we could discuss it any more, the caravan stopped. Prima opened the door and we all climbed down. I held Saturn tightly in my arms, not wanting to be parted from him again so soon.

'OMIGOD!' said Tilly.

'OMIGOD!' I said at the same time.

'*O-mi-dog!*' said Prima, and we all laughed.

We were standing outside a huge house with brick walls and a red-tiled roof. Julius and Prima led the way along a path of white marble. All along the path there were statues on tall pillars.

'This is so weird,' said Tilly. 'It's like being in a museum.'

The path led to a stone archway and we all walked through. We were in a big courtyard, with rooms leading off in every direction. Some of the doors were open and we could see that the walls were decorated with paintings and the floors were covered in intricate, colourful mosaics.

Tilly grabbed my arm and pointed. 'Can you believe it?' she said. 'They've even got a swimming pool.'

She was right. Over at one end of the courtyard was a big swimming pool. Through the clear water, I could see that it too was lined with mosaics.

'Do you think Campania might be the Latin word for Beverly Hills?' said Tilly, laughing.

Prima seemed happy with our response and she led the way round the courtyard, opening doors and pointing.

'*Culina*,' she said as she opened the door to the kitchen.

'Like culinary,' said Tilly. 'My dad boasts about his culinary skills, whenever he manages to make toast without burning it.'

Then Prima opened a door to a bedroom. '*Cubiculum*,' she said.

'Like cubicle,' I said. 'You know what, Tilly? The Romans seem to have stolen lots of our words.'

Tilly laughed. 'I think it might have been the other way round.'

She was right of course and I felt a bit stupid, but Tilly smiled at me and then I didn't feel so bad.

Soon we'd seen all the rooms and Prima led us back across the courtyard. But suddenly I noticed that Tilly wasn't smiling any more.

'What?' I asked.

'This is all lovely,' she said. 'But I wonder what the slave quarters are like? They could be totally horrible.'

'But . . .'

In all the excitement of exploring the house, I'd actually managed to forget that we were slaves.

'Julius bought us, remember?' said Tilly.

'Well, he bought me,' I corrected her. 'Technically, he stole you. You probably still belong to the ogre.'

Tilly shuddered. 'Do you think the ogre might come looking for me?'

I shook my head. 'No way. Did you see the way he sucked up to Julius? Clearly Julius is an important man and the ogre would never do anything to upset him. He won't come here searching for his runaway slave.'

'You're probably right, but it doesn't really matter who owns us. We're still slaves. I wonder what work we'll have to do?'

'Not picking onions, I hope. Trust me, Tilly, that so isn't fun.'

Tilly rolled her eyes. 'Enough with the onions already,' she said.

Prima had brought us back to one of the bedrooms, and she indicated that we should go inside.

'I suppose she wants us to tidy it for her,' I said. 'I hope she's not a slob like Amy. It would take months to clean her room properly.'

The room was big and already perfectly tidy. Prima patted a huge bed. '*Prima*,' she said.

Then she pushed open a door into a smaller room with two narrow beds. She patted each one in turn. '*Tilly . . . Lauren,*' she said.

Tilly grinned. 'I've seen wardrobes bigger than this room,' she said, 'but I'm so happy we don't have to sleep in a shed or a cave or something.'

Then Prima ran back into her own room. She returned with a beautifully embroidered pillow. She put the pillow on the floor between the two beds.

'Sattie,' she said.

Tilly put her rucksack down on her bed and I lay Saturn on his cushion, where he immediately fell asleep.

'Settle in, Lauren,' said Tilly. 'It looks like we've found a new home.'

11

We followed Prima back into her bedroom. She sat on the bed and Tilly and I sat on a bench near the wall. At first we had fun pointing at things in the room and repeating their Latin names after Prima, but that was only entertaining for a few minutes. After that, it felt a bit like being at school and I half expected Prima to start handing out gold stars to Tilly and me for being so good at our lessons.

Then the three of us sat in silence.

'This is getting a bit embarrassing,' said Tilly in the end. 'At least the last time you time-travelled, you could speak the language.'

'Yeah, I suppose that helped a bit,' I said. 'But

you'd be surprised how much stuff you and I talk about that made no sense at all to people in 1912.'

Tilly laughed. 'Do you think there's anyone around here who speaks English? These people are totally rich. Maybe we could get an interpreter.'

I shook my head. 'That wouldn't be any good. English has changed so much since the time of the Ancient Romans, we wouldn't even recognize it. My mum studied Old English in college and she says it was like a completely different language.'

'Pity we didn't bring your mum along so. Do you think we could send Saturn back to pick her up?'

'No way,' I said quickly. 'One of the best things about time travel is getting to live in a mum-free world for a little while.'

Too late, I realized what I'd said. Tilly's mum is dead and the only world she knows is a mum-free one.

'I'm so sorry, Tilly,' I said. 'I'm a complete idiot. I just meant . . . you know . . . it's kind of a novelty to be free . . . with no one warning you to wear a coat and . . . you know . . . to say please and thank you all the time and . . . stuff . . . and . . .'

I kept going, not sure if I was making things better or worse.

Tilly hugged me. 'It's fine, Lauren. I know you didn't mean to hurt me, so I'll forgive you if you promise to stop babbling.'

'Thanks,' I said as I hugged her back.

While we were talking, Prima was staring at us with a polite, frozen smile on her face.

'This is awful,' I moaned. 'It's like when Mum and Dad have people over to visit and I'm supposed to hang out with their weird children, and they act all surprised when we're not instant best friends.'

'Oh, I have an idea,' said Tilly, jumping up. 'Maybe there's something in my schoolbag that we can talk about. Should I show Prima my phone, do you think?'

I shook my head. 'Maybe that would be too much of a shock. Best to start with something a bit less high-tech.'

I could hear Tilly unzipping her schoolbag, and a second later she came back holding her history book.

'That looks like a lot of fun,' I said. 'We can have a history lesson.'

Tilly ignored my sarcastic tone.

'Trust me,' she said. 'It will work. This book's got lots of pictures.'

She sat next to Prima, and I went to sit beside them. Prima took the book from Tilly and turned it over and over in her hands. Tilly showed her how to open it and Prima ran her hands over the pages, like they were the smoothest things she had ever touched. Then she leaned forward and smelled the pages.

I giggled. 'Does she think it's something you're supposed to eat?'

Tilly giggled too. 'If she takes a bite out of my book, I'm going to have a really hard time explaining it to Mrs Simms when I get back to school.'

'Why's she acting so weird anyway? Didn't they have books in Roman times?' I asked.

'I'll tell you in a second,' said Tilly. She took the history book from Prima and flicked through it until she got to the chapter on Ancient Rome.

'Nope,' she said in the end. 'They wrote on papyrus scrolls.'

Prima took the book back from Tilly and turned the pages slowly. She especially liked the pictures of the people in the chapter on Ancient Rome. She ran her fingers over each one, almost like she knew them.

Then she turned a page and Tilly gasped. 'Saturn,' she said.

I looked through the doorway, but could see that Saturn was still asleep on his cushion.

'No,' said Tilly. 'Not that Saturn. There's one here too.'

I looked down the list of Roman gods and stopped near the end where Tilly was pointing.

'See, Lauren,' she said. 'Saturn was the Roman god of time. That's why Prima was mad earlier. Maybe using a god's name for a cat is a sign of disrespect or something.'

'The god of time,' I repeated. 'Of course. It makes perfect sense. Whoever christened Saturn knew exactly what they were doing. Who could think of a better name for a time-travelling cat?'

'Anyway, enough about cats,' said Tilly. 'Let's see what she makes of this.'

Tilly helped Prima to flick through the pages until they came to the chapter on the Second World War. Prima looked closely at the pictures of the fighter aeroplanes flying over a city, then she shook her head. Tilly pointed at the planes and flapped her arms like wings.

Prima shook her head again and closed her eyes, like she was trying to make the pictures go away. In her world, only birds could fly and clearly she couldn't imagine anything else.

She worked back through the pages until she came to the Ancient Rome section again. Then she examined the images for a long time, smiling to herself.

'No wonder Roman civilization collapsed,' said Tilly, grinning. 'They weren't ready to embrace change.'

 **12**

We looked at the history book for ages, and then the sound of a gong made Prima close the book and stand up.

Tilly and I followed Prima into the courtyard. She stopped and opened a door that led into a small room.

'What . . .?' began Tilly, wrinkling her nose.

'Oh yes,' I said, showing off. 'I forgot to tell you about the whole communal toilet thing they do around here.'

Tilly examined the line of four toilets set in a semicircle round the wall.

'That's totally gross,' she said. 'And I'm not even going to ask you what that sponge thing on a stick is used for.'

'Just as well, because I don't know,' I said. 'But I sooo don't like what I'm thinking.'

Tilly made a face.

'Back on the onion farm, the toilets seemed like the place people went for a chat,' I said.

Tilly made a worse face. 'Haven't they heard of privacy?'

'Well, Prima hasn't anyway,' I said, as Prima went to one of the toilets and began to pull up her tunic.

'My mum is always saying "When in Rome, do as the Romans do",' I said.

Tilly dragged me from the room, giggling. 'Sorry,' she said. 'This isn't Rome, remember? This is Campania, and when it comes to toilets, I'm doing as twenty-first century people do.'

As soon as Prima came out from the toilet, Tilly went in, and when she was finished I took my turn.

Prima watched as if we were crazy. Then she took us to a bathing area where we could wash our hands and faces.

Next she took us back to pick up Saturn, and then we all went to a room that had three couches arranged round a large, low table. Some of the couches were already occupied.

'*Familia*,' she said.

Julius was lying on one couch, and he smiled when he saw us.

On the next couch there was a beautiful, elegant woman. She was dressed in a long robe with a pleated skirt. Her hair was piled on her head in huge curls held in place with shiny combs. As she stood up to greet us, her jewellery jangled like a wind chime in a gentle breeze.

Prima kissed the woman, and then turned to us. '*Mater*,' she said. '*Livia*.'

'I'm guessing that Livia is her mother,' said Tilly.

Then Prima pointed to a beautiful little girl of about three who was sitting next to her mother. '*Secunda*,' she said.

Secunda smiled shyly.

Then Prima pointed at Tilly and me and said our names. Her mother smiled at us and pointed towards the empty couch.

I was about to sit down when Tilly pulled me

back. 'We're slaves, remember? We're probably not supposed to eat with the family.'

'So why is she pointing at the couch?'

'I don't know, do I? Maybe she wants us to move it out of the way or something.'

Prima saw our hesitation and began to laugh. She took Tilly's arm and led her towards the couch and gently pushed her on to it. Then Prima sat down too. Feeling more confident, I sat down next to her and waited to see what happened next.

Prima's mother clapped her hands twice and a door at the far side of the room opened. Three slaves walked in, carrying trays. When the table was piled high with food and drink, the mother clapped her hands again and two more slaves walked in. One slave played music on a thing like a miniature guitar, and the other danced. It was nice, but a bit weird.

I nudged Tilly. 'Is this the equivalent of watching TV during meals?' I said, and she laughed.

Now everyone started to reach out for food. There weren't any plates or cutlery, and everyone

89

just grabbed stuff with their hands. Soon Tilly was copying them. Hardly anything looked familiar to me, and I sooo don't like eating stuff when I don't know what it is.

I picked up a piece of bread and chewed on it, but Prima's mother saw me and waved her arms across the table, showing me the big display of food. Feeling embarrassed, I picked up the nearest thing to me. I wasn't sure what was inside, but it looked like whatever it was had been dipped in honey and rolled in poppy seeds. It looked harmless enough, and I was just bringing it to my mouth when Tilly nudged me and pointed at the food in my hand.

'I wonder if that's a deep-fried dormouse,' she said. 'They were really popular in Roman times.'

'You're joking,' I said weakly.

'Nope. But what's the big deal? You've been through all kinds of scary things in the last twenty-four hours, so don't tell me you're afraid of a tiny dead dormouse.'

'I'm not afraid of it,' I said. 'I just don't want it anywhere near my mouth, that's all.'

Tilly sighed. 'You're such a baby, Lauren,' she said. 'People get sent home from reality TV shows for that kind of behaviour. Anyway, it probably isn't a dormouse.'

That made me feel a bit better, and I was working up the courage to take a tiny nibble when she continued. 'It's probably a flamingo's tongue. The Romans loved those too.'

I was starting to feel really sick, and I had no idea what to do with the lump of food in my hand. All I knew for sure was that there was no way it was going anywhere near my lips.

Then there was a sudden, loud crash, as someone dropped something in the kitchen. Everyone turned and looked, and I quickly threw the piece of food under the table. Saturn raced over and ate it in one bite, and for the rest of the meal, I ate bread.

When the food was gone, the other slaves returned and began to clear up.

'Should we offer to help, do you think?' asked Tilly.

I shrugged. 'At home, my mum would kill me if

she thought I didn't help to clean up after a meal, but here I have no idea what to do. We're supposed to be slaves, and yet the other slaves are waiting on us.'

'Maybe if we don't act like slaves, the family will forget about it,' suggested Tilly.

That seemed like a plan, so I sat for ages wondering what was the best way not to look like a slave, even though I'd been bought and sold twice in the last twenty-four hours.

When Julius finally left the table, the rest of us got up too. Livia took Secunda to the swimming pool and watched as she splashed her feet. Saturn curled up for yet another sleep. Tilly went to our room and returned with her colouring pencils and her maths exercise book. Then she joined Prima and me in a shady corner of the courtyard.

Tilly handed the exercise book and pencils to Prima, who spent ages experimenting with different colours and patterns.

'What's the big deal?' asked Tilly. 'They're just boring old colouring pencils.'

'Can't you see?' I replied. 'It's her first time. It's like she's back in infants' class, and these pencils could well be the most exciting things she's seen in her whole life.'

'She needs to get out more,' said Tilly, and we both laughed.

By now, Prima had covered most of Tilly's maths book with coloured scribbles.

'Mrs Simms is going to kill you when she sees that,' I said. 'What are you going to tell her?'

'I'll tell her the truth. I'll tell her an Ancient Roman scribbled on it.'

We both laughed at the thought.

Tilly sighed. 'It would be the first honest excuse I've ever given her. Anyway, I'm not going to worry about that at the moment. Maths class feels like a million miles away from here right now.'

And I couldn't argue with that.

When it started to get dark, we made our way to our beds. A slave girl came to our room and lit a lamp so we could see.

I wasn't looking forward to another night sleeping in my school uniform, so I was glad when Prima dug around in a big chest and pulled out two tunics for Tilly and me to wear in bed.

When we were all settled, Prima's mother came into her room. She talked to her daughter for a while and then kissed her goodnight.

Next she came into our little room. She said a few things that we couldn't understand, then she touched each of us gently on the forehead, blew out the lamp and tiptoed out.

Tilly and I whispered together in the darkness.

'So what do you think of time travel now?' I asked.

'It's all a bit weird and scary and very tiring, but I think I like it.'

'And what do you think is going to happen tomorrow?'

'What do you mean?'

'Well, as you keep pointing out, we're slaves. All the other slaves have to work, so I don't suppose you and I will be spending tomorrow lying round the swimming pool.'

Tilly sighed. 'That's a pity. Do you think working on our tans would count as work?'

'I wish.'

From the next room, Prima called something out.

'I suppose that's Latin for Goodnight,' I said.

'Goodnight to you too, Prima,' said Tilly. 'Sleep tight and don't let the bedbugs bite.'

And seconds later I could hear her snoring peacefully.

13

I woke up to see Prima standing in the doorway, saying my name and Tilly's. It was already bright and I had a feeling that we had been asleep for a very long time.

I pulled Tilly's arm to wake her up and we both sat up in bed.

'This is it,' said Tilly. 'She's waking us up so that we can start work. If one of us has to clean those stinky toilets, how about we do rock-paper-scissors to decide who escapes?'

'That's sooo not fair,' I said. 'You always win when we do rock-paper-scissors.'

'You can't blame me for being lucky,' she said. 'I –'

She stopped talking as Prima beckoned to us to get up.

The night before, Tilly and I had thrown our clothes in a heap on the floor. I looked at my dirty, crumpled uniform and really didn't fancy another day of wearing it.

As I bent down to pick up my skirt, Prima clapped her hands and instantly a slave was beside us. Prima said something to her and the girl gathered up all of our dirty clothes and put them into a basket.

Then Prima brought us into her room and she opened a big wardrobe. Clearly she was a very spoiled girl, as the wardrobe was stuffed with clothes.

Tilly made a face. 'Where's the fun in having a gazillion outfits if they're all exactly the same?'

She was right. All of Prima's clothes seemed to be long tunic-type dresses in various not-very-exciting colours. Some were decorated on the hem, but most were plain.

Prima seemed to be waiting for a reaction.

'Wow!' I said.

'OMG!' said Tilly.

I considered we were pretty good actors, as I've seen better collections of clothes in the scabby old charity shop at the end of our road.

Prima pulled out a few tunics and held them up to us.

'What do you think?' asked Tilly. 'Should I wear the grey or the grey?'

I punched her lightly on the arm. 'Don't be such an ungrateful little slave,' I said.

In the end, Prima gave us each a pale green tunic. She also gave us each a belt to tie round our waists.

'Totally cool,' said Tilly. 'Not.'

As I put on the clothes, I felt like I was getting dressed up for a school play, and I half expected to see Mrs Simms fussing about, asking if I'd learned my lines properly.

When we were dressed, Prima sat us on her bed and took a wooden box from her wardrobe. When she opened it, Tilly and I gasped – and this time we weren't faking it.

The box was piled high with bangles and neck-pieces.

'These are all made of silver,' I said, as I ran my fingers along one beautiful bracelet.

Tilly let a delicate chain slide through her fingers. 'If we brought one of these home, we could make a fortune,' she said.

'Tilly!' I said, shocked. 'That would be stealing.'

'Would it? Maybe I'd be helping the study of world history. And Prima wouldn't even miss one bangle – she's got heaps.'

'Well, I wouldn't have anything to do with it,' I said primly. 'Handling stolen goods is wrong.'

'Don't touch me then,' said Tilly. 'I am stolen goods, remember?'

I leaned over and touched her arm and Tilly pointed at me accusingly – 'Criminal, criminal,' she chanted.

We were both laughing by now, thinking we were being very funny.

Then Prima leaned over and touched Tilly's shoulder. 'Cri-ni-mal,' she chanted, smiling.

Clearly she thought we were playing some weird game, or engaging in some kind of tribal dance from our native land.

The three of us chanted until our throats were sore, and then we collapsed on to Prima's bed, laughing.

When we had recovered, Prima reached into her jewellery box and picked out two silver bangles. She held them towards Tilly and me.

'Do you think she wants us to clean them for her or something?' asked Tilly.

Before I could answer, Prima gave each of us a bangle.

'Wow,' said Tilly. 'I wish we knew the Latin for *thank you.*'

But we didn't, so we both smiled and tried to use our faces to show how grateful we were.

Then I had an idea. I held my own charm bracelet towards Tilly. 'Help me to take off a charm,' I said. 'I'd like to give one to Prima.'

'Which one?'

I had to think for ages. Each charm told a story

and seemed to be part of my life. I ran my fingers over the medal Mary had given me, the cat that reminded me of Saturn and the tiny *Titanic*. Finally I settled on the small silver flower with the tiny yellow crystal in the centre.

'But your mum and dad gave you that,' said Tilly.

'I know. But they'll understand – I think.'

Tilly unclipped the charm and we slipped it on to one of Prima's chains. I held it towards Prima and she took it and fastened it round her neck.

'*Benigne*,' she said.

'*Benigne*,' said Tilly and I together, pointing to our new bangles.

Then Prima indicated that we should go and eat, and we followed her from the room.

'I wonder what we're going to do today,' I said, as we followed Prima across the courtyard.

Tilly shrugged. 'Who cares? Prima's let us sleep near her. She's given us her clothes and her jewellery. She's not going to make us act like real slaves after all of that. She's treating us like friends. So let's enjoy ourselves.'

I knew she was right and I felt very happy and adventurous as we joined the rest of the family for breakfast.

 **14**

'Don't you think that guy's totally cute?' said
Tilly, after a slave had poured us each a jug
of delicious juice. 'His name is Felix. I heard Prima
saying it earlier.'

Tilly was right – Felix was totally cute. He was tall
and thin, with perfect skin and huge dark eyes.

'Do you think he likes me?' asked Tilly.

I shook my head. 'Sorry, Tilly. Haven't you seen
the way he looks at Prima? It's obvious that he
adores her.'

She looked at him again and sighed. 'You're
right. I'd hoped I was imagining that.'

'The poor boy,' I said. 'Prima's the pampered
daughter of the house. No slave boy, no matter

how handsome, is ever going to have a chance
with her.'

After breakfast, Tilly and I went back to the
courtyard and sat on a seat outside Prima's room.

'Maybe we'll get to go to school today,' I said.
'Wouldn't that be totally fun?'

'For someone who seems to like school so much,'
said Tilly, 'you don't seem that familiar with what's
inside your history book.'

'What do you mean?'

'Girls of Prima's age don't go to school any more.
They just hang around the house, waiting to get
married.'

As she spoke, Secunda and Prima came along.
Prima was holding something that looked like a
miniature blackboard covered with a layer of wax. I
pointed at the blackboard and looked at Prima with
my best questioning face.

She showed us a pencil-shaped piece of metal.

'*Stilus*,' she said.

Tilly collapsed into a fit of giggles. '*Stilus*,' she

repeated. 'This is historic, Lauren. We're looking at the first ever DS.'

We got over our laughing and the four of us sat on the grass. Prima used her *stilus* to write on the waxy surface of the board. When she made a mistake, she used the flat end of the stilus to rub it out. Then we played a game of writing words and drawing pictures. Secunda drew a little dog, and Prima wrote *canis*. Then I drew a horse and Prima wrote *equus*.

'Like *equestrian*!' said Tilly. 'I am so going to take up Latin next year. I'll be fluent in a few weeks.'

Soon, the blackboard was full of drawings and writing.

'Oh dear,' said Tilly. 'Design flaw. How do we get it smooth again?'

In answer, Prima clapped her hands. A slave appeared and took the blackboard away. When she returned a few minutes later, the wax had been heated and our writing had disappeared. All we had to do was wait for it to harden and we could start all over again.

'Magic,' said Tilly. 'We've just seen the world's first Etch A Sketch!'

A short while later, Prima took us to a big airy room where her mother was waiting. They spent ages and ages combing each other's hair and rubbing scented lotions into each other's skin.

'Do they do this every day?' I asked.

Tilly shrugged. 'Probably. After all, in a world without TV, you have to find something to pass the time.'

Prima and her mother sat and sewed for a while. Then a slave came in and tried to teach Prima to play a long wooden wind instrument. Prima was useless, but the poor slave had to keep smiling and encouraging her, even though the sharp screechy sound she was making must have hurt his ears.

After that, we had a swim. Well, Tilly and I had a swim. Prima just sat at the edge, backing away whenever it looked like she might get splashed.

'I can't believe it,' said Tilly, when she stopped to

rest after doing about twenty lengths of the pool.
'Prima seems to be afraid of the water.'

She was right. 'What a waste,' I said. 'Imagine
having a swimming pool in your garden and being
too scared to use it.'

Tilly sighed as she lay on the grass, letting the sun
warm her skin.

'This is perfect,' she said. 'Do you think if I clap
my hands, a slave might bring me a nice cold drink
and a few crisps?'

'Mmmm,' I said. 'That sounds great. Maybe –'

Then I stopped myself. Tilly and I both know that
slavery is totally wrong, but already we were starting
to act like it was normal – like it was OK for one
person to own another.

Tilly was looking at me guiltily and I knew she
was thinking the same thing.

Before we could discuss it, though, Prima's
mother was calling us again and it was time for
lunch.

After lunch, we all lay on couches and listened to
some slaves who seemed to be reciting poetry. Felix

was there and he performed last. He stood and stared at Prima with his huge eyes and recited what I hoped was a love poem.

'That's the saddest thing ever,' sighed Tilly. 'He's repeating the words of some poet guy because he'll never be allowed to say what he really thinks. The poor boy is going to die of unrequited love.'

I thought maybe she was right. All the way through his recital, Prima had looked bored – like she couldn't wait for him to finish.

I wished I could talk to Felix and console him, but there was nothing I could do, so I helped myself to more grapes and tried not to feel too mean.

When I was in bed that night, with Saturn curled up by my feet, Tilly and I whispered for a long time.

'We're not being treated like slaves, so why do you think Prima's father brought us here?' I asked.

'I've been wondering that too,' said Tilly. 'Maybe he saw that we were foreigners and thought that we could teach Prima our language.'

'That was a bit of a waste,' I said. 'Even if we did

manage to teach her our language, poor Prima wouldn't have anyone else to speak to in English for hundreds of years.'

'I've been thinking about this whole time-travel thing,' said Tilly. 'Are we supposed to make a difference to someone's life while we're here? Are we meant to change the world?'

'What do you mean?'

'Well, when you were on the *Titanic*, you helped Mary to save herself.'

'Possibly,' I said. 'I'd like to think that I helped her, but I'll never know for sure.'

'But this time you've picked a few onions, and I helped Prima with her sewing while her mother wasn't looking, but that's hardly earth-shattering stuff, is it?'

'No. Maybe we should organize an anti-slavery march or something,' I suggested. 'We could make banners and –'

'No way!' said Tilly quickly. 'It's a noble idea, but I think it might be the kind of noble idea that could get us into an awful lot of trouble. Slavery is wrong, but I've a funny feeling that the Ancient Romans aren't ready to face up to that fact.'

I knew she was right.

'So, do you want to go back home?' I asked.

She thought for a while. 'I kind of do and I kind of don't. What about you?'

'Well, I miss home and I miss my family, and I'm a bit worried about my schoolbag, which is on the grass in front of my house, but . . .'

'But what?'

'But it's kind of nice being here.'

Tilly sighed. 'Yes, it is kind of nice here.'

'And who else do we know who will ever get a chance to spend time in Ancient Rome?'

She laughed. 'And you're sure that time isn't passing at home?'

'I think I'm sure. Last time I was gone for days and days, but only minutes passed at home. And besides, don't you ever read fantasy books? People vanish for years and still get home in time for tea.'

'But this isn't fantasy. This is real. And then

there's another thing – can we trust Saturn to bring us back when we need him to?'

I hesitated. This was the part I was most unsure of. Last time when I'd begged Saturn to take me home, he'd done as I asked. But maybe that was just luck, or coincidence, or something I had no control over.

'Er . . . yes . . . sort of . . . maybe,' I said. 'But it's not like we can do a practice run. If we get him to take us home, how could we trust him to bring us back to this very time and place?'

Tilly shuddered. 'We couldn't. We might end up back in the ogre's clutches, and I so wouldn't fancy that.'

'So how about we stay here for another while, and when we've had enough, we'll ask Saturn to take us home?'

Tilly sat up and stroked Saturn's head. 'We can trust you, Saturn, can't we?'

In reply, Saturn stretched and miaowed loudly, and Tilly and I laughed and settled down to sleep.

15

After breakfast the next day, instead of taking us to her mother's room, Prima led us out under the arch. Felix was outside with the two horses and the caravan.

'Satur . . . I mean Sattie?' I said to Prima.

I had no idea where we were going, or how long we were going to be, and parting from Saturn always makes me nervous when I'm years away from home.

But Prima just smiled and shook her head and said something that I totally hoped meant that we wouldn't be gone for long.

I ran back and got Tilly's schoolbag, and then we all climbed into the caravan.

'Yay,' said Tilly as we set off. 'We're going on a road trip.'

A while later, we stopped near the centre of the city. Felix waited in the shade, minding the horses and the caravan while the rest of us went off exploring.

Prima took us to a place where the streets were narrow and cobbled. There were heaps of little shops that sold all kinds of amazing stuff. At one shop, Prima bought cakes filled with honey, and in another she bought us each a drink. Prima bought herself a whole bag full of jewellery and tiny bottles of perfume. Then she bought Tilly a pretty comb to hold back her hair. Finally, she led the way to a shop that sold tiny silver ornaments. Prima spoke to the shopkeeper for a long time. In the end, she grabbed my arm and showed my charm bracelet to the shopkeeper.

'OMIGOD,' I gasped. 'She's trying to sell my bracelet to this man.'

'Look on the bright side,' said Tilly. 'At least she's not trying to sell you.'

I needn't have worried, though. The shopkeeper dug around in some baskets behind the counter and finally pulled out something that he handed to Prima. She opened her palm and showed it to me. It was a girl in a Roman tunic, just like the one I was wearing. I stroked the tiny figure.

'It's just perfect,' I sighed.

Prima paid the man and then held my arm towards him. He fixed the charm on to my bracelet in the gap where the flower used to be.

'Benigne,' I said to Prima, and she smiled.

We walked through the streets for a long time. Prima pointed at things and spoke to us in Latin.

'Prima's talking to us a lot more today,' said Tilly after a while. 'I don't know why she bothers, as we barely understand a word she says.'

'Maybe she thinks we're like babies and that if she talks for long enough, eventually we'll become fluent.'

'If that's so, she kind of has a point, but that would take years and years, and we're not exactly planning on hanging around that long, are we?'

Suddenly I felt sorry for Prima. She was a friendly, generous girl. She was being really nice to us, and she probably thought we were going to stay with her forever. How could she know that Tilly and I were just having a bit of fun, and that far away, in another place and time, we had real lives and real families waiting for us to come back?

'Let's not think about that now,' I said quickly. 'Let's just enjoy our day out.'

Sometime later, we were wandering down a narrow lane, with Prima leading the way as usual, when Tilly called my name in the weirdest, croaky voice.

I looked to where she was pointing and felt suddenly sick. It was the ogre, grinning his evil grin and walking right towards us.

There was no time to warn Prima. There was no time to discuss the finer points of who belonged to Prima's family and who belonged to the ogre. There was only time for me to say, 'Run!' before I turned and, with Tilly on my heels, I sprinted as fast as I could.

I pushed past shoppers and children, soldiers and workers; I scrambled through flocks of chickens and ducks; I elbowed through a pair of elderly donkeys and I jumped over a sick-looking dog. I'd been caught by the ogre once before, and I sooo wasn't going to let that happen again.

Finally, when I couldn't run any more, I threw myself into a narrow gap between two tall buildings and made room for Tilly to squash in beside me.

For ages, we said nothing as we struggled to catch our breath.

Finally Tilly peeped round the corner. 'It's OK, Lauren,' she said. 'We've shaken him off. Everything's fine.'

'Do you know where Prima is?' I asked.

Tilly shook her head.

'Do you think you could find the caravan?'

Another shake.

'Or Prima's house?'

Shake.

'Or Saturn?'

She shook her head one more time.

'And everything's fine?'

'Well, the ogre didn't catch us, so we're not one step away from being onion-farmers for the rest of our lives. All we have to do is find Prima and then we'll be grand. Like I said – everything's fine. Sort of.'

16

We walked for ages and ages. All the streets looked the same and I had a horrible feeling that we were walking round in circles. We had no idea where we were going, or what we were going to do. I had left Tilly's schoolbag in the caravan, so we didn't have her history book with us to check the facts. It didn't matter, though. I didn't need a book to tell me that people in Roman times probably weren't very nice to runaway slaves.

'Poor Prima,' I said after a while.

Tilly gave a grim laugh. 'Poor Prima? She knows the way home. And her dad can buy her two more slaves tomorrow. After a few days, we could be slaving in a salt mine or something, and Prima will have forgotten we ever existed. We're nothing to her.'

'That's not true,' I protested. 'We do mean something to her. She's been really kind. She bought us presents and shared her clothes with us. And now she'll think we're ungrateful little pigs who just ran off on her.'

Tilly sighed. 'You're right. Prima has been extra nice to us – and she might even be worried about us. But given a choice, I'd rather be her than us right now.'

And I couldn't argue with that.

Much later, we were still lost. We were also tired, and hungry and thirsty. We heard a crowd cheering and I realized that we were walking past a huge amphitheatre.

'Was there a colosseum in Campania?' asked Tilly. 'And do you think that might be it?'

'You're supposed to be the history expert,' I said. 'But there's definitely something happening in there.

Pity there's not a sign and a board in lights to tell us what's on today.'

'Should we go in for a look?'

I shook my head. 'No! We're runaway slaves.'

'Technically, I'm the only runaway. You're just lost.'

'Do you fancy trying to explain the difference to a sword-wielding Roman who doesn't speak our language and thinks we should be gladiators?'

'Er, maybe not.'

Tilly allowed me to pull her away and we walked on for another while.

Soon we were so tired we couldn't walk any more and I was very close to tears. Even though Tilly was trying to be brave, I was fairly sure she felt exactly the same as I did.

'I wish Saturn was with us,' I said for the hundredth time. 'This would be a really good time to ask him to take us back home.'

'What happens if we never go back home?' wailed Tilly.

'I've been wondering that too,' I said. 'But time

travel is kind of complicated, and I'm not exactly an expert.'

'So what are we going to do?'

'I was hoping you had an idea.'

She shook her head. 'I'm all out of ideas. I –'

'Tilly!' I screeched.

She grabbed my arm.

'What is it? Who is it? Is it the ogre? Where is he?'

She followed my gaze and then gave a big, happy sigh.

Felix was walking towards us with a huge smile on his face. I'm not sure what the etiquette about hugging slaves is, but right then I didn't care. I raced over and hugged him tightly, stopping only when Tilly pushed me away so she could hug him too.

'Are you hugging him because he's going to rescue us, or because you fancy him?' I asked when she finally let go.

Tilly went red. 'Maybe a bit of both,' she said.

Then we followed Felix, and after only a few

121

minutes we were back at the caravan. Felix tapped on the door and Prima came out.

Her eyes were red and her face was streaked with tears. Tilly and I hugged her and we tried to explain what had happened. I got out one of Tilly's exercise books and drew a picture of the scariest man I could, brandishing a sword. In front of him, I drew Tilly and me running away from him.

'Prima doesn't seem to understand,' I said. 'I wonder why?'

'Maybe because that looks just like my hockey coach when we aren't playing well enough for him,' said Tilly, giggling.

Tilly took the exercise book from me, and even though her picture was quite good, I had to get back at her, so I said hers looked like my dad doing a spot of gardening on a Sunday afternoon.

In the end, I had no idea if Prima understood what we were trying to say, but she seemed glad to see us and that was good enough for me.

She pointed to a stone jar containing cool water

in a basket in the caravan, and Felix poured us all a
drink before we climbed back in.

'I've had a very long day,' said Tilly. 'I hope we're
going back to the villa.'

'Me too,' I said. 'Home sweet home.'

 **17**

When the caravan stopped, we were on the side of the hill that I'd seen from Prima's house.

We climbed out and looked around. It was a beautiful place. The hill was lined with fields of lemon and olive trees. We could see the city spread out in front of us, and in the distance the sea sparkled in the sunlight.

Tilly sighed. 'This has to be the most perfect, peaceful place on earth. Prima's lucky to live here.'

Felix brought blankets from the caravan, and spread them on the ground in the shade of a huge tree. Then, while Prima, Tilly and I sat down and admired the view, he spread out a picnic.

'The food here's OK,' said Tilly, as she stuffed her

face with cheese and bread and cold meat. 'But how come we've never had proper Italian food? How come there's no pizza, or bolognaise, or carbonara?'

'How am I supposed to know?' I said. 'Maybe they haven't been invented yet.'

When we'd finished eating, Felix took out his musical instruments and played some music. Tilly pulled her tin whistle from the bottom of her schoolbag and played two tunes. They must have sounded a bit weird to Felix and Prima, but they clapped politely and smiled.

Then Felix gathered up the picnic stuff and carried it back to the caravan.

Tilly put her tin whistle back into her bag.

'Do you think Ancient Rome is ready for this?' she said, as she pulled out her mobile phone.

She handed the phone to Prima, who looked at it for a long time. She turned it over and over in her hands. She rubbed her fingers gently over the buttons.

Tilly took the phone back and switched it on. She looked at the screen. 'Still no network available,' she said. 'I wish the Romans would get their act

125

together and put up a few mobile phone masts.'

She put on a Tetris game and tried to show Prima how it worked, but failed miserably. Prima kept trying to catch the falling shapes with her fingers, squealing whenever the phone made a noise.

'Give it to me for a sec,' I said in the end. 'Let's try something different.'

Tilly handed the phone to me and I went to the ringtones page. I pressed a button and a tinkly version of 'We Wish You a Merry Christmas' washed over the hillside.

Prima jumped to her feet in surprise, and Felix came running over to see what was happening.

Tilly and I laughed. Then Tilly handed the phone back to Prima and showed her how to scroll down to hear different tunes.

Prima beamed, and after a few minutes, she handed the phone to Felix. Felix was clumsy at first, but quickly got the hang of it. Then he kept going back to what appeared to be his favourite tune. Soon Tilly and I were singing along – 'Don't worry, Be Happy'.

'That poor boy,' said Tilly after the tenth time he'd played it. 'Has he any idea what he's listening to? He's a slave in Roman times. How can he not worry? How can he be happy?'

I smiled at her. 'I'm a slave in Roman times, and right now I'm happy.'

'That is sooo different,' said Tilly.

Before I could answer, the music stopped in mid-tune. Felix shook the phone gently and held it to his ear, but not surprisingly, nothing happened.

Tilly took the phone and glanced at the screen. 'I wonder what's the Latin for "I think the battery's dead and I seem to have left my charger in another millennium"?' she said.

I didn't answer. Back when I was on the *Titanic*, I was very upset when my phone's battery died, but here on this pleasant, peaceful hillside, with Tilly, Prima and Felix, it didn't really seem like such a big deal.

A dead mobile phone wasn't interesting even to Ancient Romans, and soon Felix went and sat on a narrow stone wall and looked out over the sea. To our surprise, Prima went and sat next to him, and minutes later they were deep in conversation. Their faces were just centimetres apart and they were gazing steadily into each other's eyes.

'OMIGOD,' I said. 'She likes him. She really, really likes him. She was only pretending to be bored when Felix was reciting that poetry.'

'That's sooo romantic,' said Tilly. 'Prima's parents wouldn't approve, so she has to pretend not to notice him, even though they're madly in love.'

'And she had to pretend she wanted to show us the sights of Campania, when what she really wanted was to spend time with Felix away from her parents' prying eyes.'

'It's like Romeo and Juliet!'

'I think Romeo and Juliet ended kind of badly,' I said.

Tilly looked at Felix and Prima, who seemed so happy and so right together.

'Then it's not like Romeo and Juliet,' she said firmly. 'It's like . . . well, I don't know exactly; it's like some love story that has a happy-ever-after ending.'

*

It was nearly dark when we got back to Prima's place. Felix took the horses round to the stables at the back of the house, and the rest of us went inside. Prima's parents were sitting in the courtyard. Prima went and kissed them, looking like the perfect, obedient daughter.

'They're probably planning to marry her off to some boring old senator or something,' said Tilly. 'What would they say if they knew she was hanging out with the staff?'

'I sooo don't want to think about that,' I said. 'I'm kind of glad we don't have a language in common. At least Prima's parents can't ask us any awkward questions.'

When we went to bed that evening, Saturn was already curled up on his cushion on the floor.

'You'd never believe the day we had,' I said, but he didn't seem to care. He just blinked once and fell asleep, and seconds later, Tilly and I did the exact same thing.

18

We stayed at home for the next few days, and I was happy about that. Our day out had been fun, but it had also been totally scary and I wanted a few days with nothing more worrying than strange food to bother me.

The time passed quickly. We hung around the house and did sewing and music and stuff. Sometimes we played with Secunda and sometimes we swam in the pool. It was like a very weird, very relaxing holiday.

Then one afternoon, we were sitting in the shade of the courtyard. Tilly was helping Prima to unravel mistakes in her sewing and I was playing with Secunda, when all of a sudden, I felt slightly dizzy.

It was like I'd just stepped off a boat and the ground was swaying under my feet.

'Did you feel that?' I said to Tilly.

She looked up from her sewing.

'So you felt it too?'

'Omigod,' I said. 'Where's Saturn? Are we going back home?'

Tilly pointed to where Saturn was asleep under a chair.

'I know I haven't done a whole lot of time-travelling,' she said, 'but that didn't feel anything like a time-travel episode. That just felt weird.'

She tapped Prima on the arm and waved her fingers in the air. Prima smiled and went back to her sewing.

'If Prima's not worried, then I suppose we shouldn't be worried either, right?' said Tilly.

'Right,' I said.

But a second later, the same thing happened again, and this time Saturn miaowed loudly and leapt into my arms.

Tilly raced over and hugged me. 'Don't go

without me, Lauren,' she said. 'I so wouldn't like to be stuck here on my own.'

'And I so wouldn't like to have to explain to your dad that I'd lost you in Ancient Roman times,' I said.

But ten minutes later, we hadn't gone anywhere. The sun was still shining, Saturn was curled up asleep and the birds were singing.

Everything was perfect.

Wasn't it?

But the next day, the same rocking thing happened during dinner. Tilly nudged me and we both watched as a bowl of jelly trembled in front of us, like it was afraid of something.

'What do you think might be happening?' I said to Tilly.

She shrugged. 'Maybe they're building a new road or an aqueduct or something and it's making the ground shake.'

'But what if it isn't that?'

'You worry too much, Lauren,' she said. 'Look around you. No one's worried except for you.'

She was right. Julius was talking to Livia. Prima was feeding salad to Secunda and the slaves were slaving away as usual.

The next day was bright and sunny, just like all the days we'd spent in Roman times. I was getting a bit bored and was kind of hoping we might go out somewhere, but after breakfast, we followed Prima to her mother's room.

'Yay!' said Tilly. 'Looks like we're going to have another fun day of embroidery.'

I'd been reading more of the history book.

'You know girls here get married in their early teens,' I said. 'At least Prima will be able to escape soon.'

'Yeah, but she won't be escaping with Felix, will she? What will poor Felix do without her? And what will she do without Felix?'

We'd been paying more attention since our big day out, and we kept coming across Prima and Felix whispering in corners and smiling over private jokes.

'I wish we could do something to help them,' I said.

Tilly sighed. 'So do I, but you might as well put it out of your mind. We're slaves, we don't speak the language and any minute we could wake up and find that we're thousands of years away from here. There's nothing we can do.'

I knew she was right, but that didn't make me feel any better.

We did some more embroidery and then we had to endure Prima's music lesson.

'This is no fun,' said Tilly, when the awful screeching noise had stopped and we could talk again. 'We do the same thing every single day.'

I agreed. I wasn't sure I could face too much more of this boring existence.

'Should we think about trying to get back home?' I said.

Tilly nodded. 'I'm thinking that too. Let's just stay one more day and try to remember stuff.'

'What do you mean "remember stuff"?'

She grinned. 'If it's still Friday when we get back, we're going to have to do that history project, and we could do it on the Ancient Romans. We'll be able to get top marks without even opening a book, or switching on our computers!'

I thought about it. It *would* be stupid to waste this opportunity.

'One more day,' I agreed. 'One more day and we're out of here.'

After lunch, Prima, Tilly and I went to sit in an outside garden overlooking the sea and the city. Prima was pretending to teach us the names of the flowers in the garden, but we knew the real reason we were there. Felix was nearby, mending the wheel of the caravan, and he and Prima kept giving each other soppy, loving looks.

'Oh, look, Lauren,' said Tilly after a while. 'There's a fire over there on the hill where we had the picnic the other day.'

I looked to where she was pointing and gasped.

Suddenly it was as if I'd been looking at life through a fogged-up window, but now the fog was gone and everything was clear.

Much too clear.

'O-mi-god!' I said.

'What?' said Tilly calmly. 'Have you broken a fingernail or something?'

'This is serious,' I said. 'Look at all that smoke and ash. It's just like the picture in our geography book. You know, Tilly, I don't think that's an ordinary hill. I think it might be a volcano.'

'Cool,' said Tilly. 'I've never seen a volcano before. It's lucky there aren't any planes to be grounded by the ash cloud. Maybe progress isn't always a good thing. Maybe –'

Then she saw the look on my face and she stopped talking.

'I have a horrible feeling that city down there might be . . .' I began. I was so scared, I couldn't get the last word out, but one look at Tilly's face told me that she knew exactly what I was thinking.

'It's . . .' she said.

'It's . . .' I said.

And finally we found the strength to say it together.

'It's Pompeii!'

19

A few minutes later, Tilly and I were still hugging each other and trying to stop shaking.

'Maybe we're wrong,' said Tilly, pulling away from me. 'When we asked Prima what this place was called she said it was Campania.'

'That might be the name of the region or something,' I said. 'And anyway, who cares what the city is called? I bet that volcano is called Vesuvius, and if it is, we're in a whole lot of trouble.'

'I don't know much about it,' said Tilly. 'The story of Pompeii isn't in our history book.'

'I know heaps,' I said. 'Dad read a book about Pompeii once when we were on holiday, and he kept telling us all about it. It was totally boring.'

137

'But you listened anyway, right?'

'Well, sort of. I can remember him telling us that for days before Vesuvius erupted, there were warning signs, but everyone ignored them.'

'That could have been the weird shaking we've felt over the past few days,' said Tilly. 'That must have been a sign, and I'm so not ignoring it. We have to get out of here. There's no time to waste.'

'That's for sure,' I said. 'Anyone who delayed got buried by the ash, and that doesn't sound like much fun.'

'So where do we go?'

'That bit I remember,' I said. 'Most people who got away, escaped by boat. We have to get to the harbour.'

'So what are we waiting for?'

We both jumped up and ran over to Prima. I knew she couldn't understand me, but I babbled away desperately anyway.

'It's a volcano,' I said. 'It's going to erupt any minute! Get your parents and Secunda. Tell them it's an emergency. Tell them we have to go *immediately*. If we don't leave right this minute we're going to end up lying in the streets for tourists to take pictures of in a few thousand years' time when cameras have been invented.'

While I was talking I was waving desperately towards the smoking volcano, but Prima didn't seem to understand.

'Tell her, Felix,' I said. 'She'll do anything you say.'

Felix looked up when he heard his name, but unfortunately he didn't understand me either and he quickly turned back to fixing the caravan wheel.

'Let's try Julius and Livia,' said Tilly.

We each grabbed one of Prima's arms, and Prima let herself be pulled to the courtyard where her parents and little sister were sitting in the shade.

While Tilly tried to explain, I grabbed an exercise book and a colouring pencil and began to draw. I drew the volcano spewing smoke and ash. I drew Pompeii with collapsed buildings. I drew lots of little stick figures lying in the streets. It was like the most bizarre game of Pictionary ever. Except when time ran out there was going to be a lot more to lose than a silly game.

Everyone obeyed Julius, so I knew he was the one I had to convince. I handed my picture to him and waited.

Julius looked at the paper and suddenly he seemed to understand. He clapped his hands. A group of slaves appeared and Julius spoke quickly. The slaves stood there looking worried. Then one ran for the door and the others quickly followed.

'Phew,' I said. 'Now let's get going.'

But Prima's mother had picked up a basket and was filling it with silver cups and ornaments. Julius had gathered up some scrolls and was putting them into a large canvas bag. Neither of them was moving with any sense of urgency. They looked like they had all the time in the world.

'No!' I shouted. 'Leave that stuff. Leave everything. The archaeologists can find it in a few thousand years. We have to go *now*!'

Tilly put her hand on my shoulder. 'You're

wasting your breath, Lauren,' she said. 'They love their stuff and are afraid to leave it behind.'

'But . . .'

'They don't know what we know. To them, Pompeii is just an ordinary town and Vesuvius is just a hill.'

I nodded, suddenly understanding. 'It's like when I was on the *Titanic* – everyone except me thought it was just a big fancy ship.'

Tilly sighed. 'Exactly. We have to think of a way to make Julius and Livia see that there's no time to save anything except themselves.'

'And how are we going to do that?'

'I'm thinking. And while I'm thinking, you'd better look after Saturn.'

I turned round to see Saturn huddled in a scared-looking heap under a big stone bench.

'Sorry, Saturn,' I said, as I picked him up. 'But it's your own fault for always landing me in such dangerous places.'

I grabbed Tilly's schoolbag and put Saturn inside, zipping it almost closed so all I could see were his nose and his wide, odd eyes. I kissed his nose once and then put the schoolbag over my shoulders.

Prima's parents were still pottering around like they were getting ready to go on holiday and their plane wasn't due to leave for hours.

Tilly grabbed my arm. 'I have an idea,' she said, 'but there's no time to explain. When I give the signal, just run as quickly as you can. We need to go outside and follow the path down the hill until we get to the harbour. Do you know the way?'

I nodded. 'But we can't leave these people here. How are we going to make them follow us?'

'We make them follow by taking something precious with us.'

I looked around the room, wondering which of the lavish ornaments was the most valuable, but then I realized I was on completely the wrong track.

Tilly was walking slowly across the room.

'Hey, Secunda,' she said. 'I know you're a big girl, but I'm going to pick you up and carry you for a bit, OK?'

As Secunda grinned at her, Tilly scooped her up

and ran for the door. The sudden movement frightened Secunda and she screamed loudly.

I still couldn't speak Latin, but I was guessing she was saying something like 'Someone come here quickly and rescue me from this crazy girl!'

'Perfect, Secunda,' said Tilly. 'Scream as loudly as you can.'

As if she understood, Secunda screamed again. Tilly raced out through the door, across the courtyard and through the archway. I followed as Tilly scrambled across the gravel towards the path to the harbour. In her arms, Secunda was white-faced, probably too scared to scream any more.

Ahead of us, I could see some people hurrying in the direction of the sea. After a minute, I looked back and saw that we were being followed by Julius, Livia and Prima. The element of surprise had given Tilly and me a good head start, and we were well out of their reach.

'Felix isn't with them,' said Tilly.

I'd noticed that too, but knew there was nothing

we could do about it. If we ran back for him, we'd probably all be killed.

'Don't worry,' I said, trying to sound confident. 'He's probably not far behind them.'

Before Tilly could reply, there was a loud grumbling noise. I looked across at Vesuvius and saw that it was now puffing out huge clouds of ash and stones. The peaceful hillside of a few days earlier was impossible to imagine now.

Crowds of people began to push past us, even faster than before, and it was hard to keep steady on the rough path.

Soon we were being showered with ash. Secunda wasn't struggling any more. She was clinging on to Tilly like her life depended on it – and it probably did.

Tilly was tiring, though, and had slowed to a kind of stumbling walk. Before long, Julius was next to us, but that didn't matter now. Tilly's plan had worked.

Julius was leaning over to take Secunda from Tilly's arms when a sudden shower of rocks and pebbles descended on top of us.

'*Look out!*' I screamed.

Tilly jumped out of the way, but Julius was too late. A huge rock hit him on the leg, and even though I'd never witnessed anything like it before, I had a horrible feeling that I'd just heard the sound of a bone being broken.

Julius collapsed on to the ground, moaning. His tanned face had turned the dull white colour of his toga. Livia pulled desperately at his arm, but Julius couldn't stand up. He waved towards the harbour, indicating that we should leave him, but Livia refused. Julius turned to Prima and shouted something, but Prima just sat down beside him and folded her arms. Secunda clung to Livia's legs and silent tears poured down her cheeks. Julius put his face in his hands and moaned again.

Tilly and I stared at each other.

'We've got to go, Lauren,' she said.

'But we can't leave them,' I protested. 'They'll die up here.'

'If we stay, we'll all die,' she replied quietly.

This was much too big a decision for me.

Sometimes I can't even decide what kind of cereal to have for breakfast, or what colour toothbrush to buy. How was I supposed to figure this out?

Then I saw Prima jump to her feet, with a huge smile on her face. I turned to see Felix galloping towards us on one of the big white horses. He stopped beside us and jumped to the ground.

Tilly held the horse, stroking its nose and whispering to try to calm it down. Prima, Felix and I pulled and dragged and struggled until we had managed to hoist Julius over the horse's back. The poor man didn't look very dignified, with his hair all messed up and his bottom in the air, but I suspect he didn't care.

Then we continued our journey.

 **20**

When we finally got to the harbour, there was total chaos, as crowds of people cried and pushed and shoved. There were regular showers of ash and rocks – each one followed by a fresh chorus of screams. The air smelled bad, like someone had set off a hundred stink bombs. Some people had pillows and thick blankets over their heads to protect themselves from the falling debris.

Luckily there was a big fleet of boats waiting to help us. When we got to one with space, a group of soldiers came and carried Julius on board and the rest of us followed. Felix patted the horse on its rump and set it free to try to save itself. Then he came on board too.

But the boat still hadn't moved ten minutes later, as crowds of people tried to force their way aboard.

Julius lay on a bench. His face had turned grey now, and clearly he was in a lot of pain. Prima's mother sat next to him, rubbing his forehead and whispering to him. Secunda clutched her mother's tunic and sobbed quietly. I couldn't see where Felix had gone.

Prima, Tilly and I were all pushed together on the other side of the deck, near the wooden railings. The three of us held hands, and I hoped the others wouldn't notice how badly mine were shaking. On my back, through Tilly's schoolbag, I could feel Saturn's gentle breathing. I very much wanted to take him out and cuddle him, but I was too afraid. Things were scary enough already, and if Saturn ran off, I wasn't sure I could cope.

'Phew,' said Tilly. 'At last we're safe. That could all have turned out really –'

Before she could finish the sentence, a huge wave rocked the boat. Everyone screamed and there was a surge of people towards our side of the deck. A

148

tall man stumbled and while trying to save himself, his two outstretched arms hit Prima.

And then everything seemed to happen in slow motion.

I held on as tightly as I could, but Prima's hand slipped from mine.

She grabbed for the railings – and missed. Her mouth opened, but no sound came out, as she overbalanced slowly and then tumbled downwards. Her tunic fluttered briefly, and then I watched in horror as my friend vanished slowly under the rough, grey water.

'*Prima!*' I screeched.

I grabbed a man near me. 'Help her! You've got to help my friend!' I yelled. 'She's afraid of water. She can't swim.'

The man looked worried, but he didn't do anything. He just held tighter to his wife and baby. I had a horrible feeling that he'd have ignored me even if I'd spoken a language he could understand.

Tilly was pulling off her shoes. 'I'm probably the best swimmer here,' she said. 'I can save her.'

Tilly is a great swimmer, but I've never seen her swim in a rough sea, with a huge boat bobbing next to her and a volcano spitting ash and gravel everywhere.

How could I let her risk her life? How could I not let her try to save Prima?

'Be careful,' was all I could say as Tilly climbed on to the wooden railing.

And then there was another shout. A figure grabbed Tilly and pulled her back so that she fell to the deck in a heap. Then the figure climbed on to the railing, and a second later, he had vanished in a graceful dive.

I helped Tilly to her feet. She was a bit dazed. 'Who was that?' she asked.

'Felix,' I said. 'It was Felix.'

We watched as Prima bobbed to the surface again – and as her arms went round Felix's neck.

Tilly sighed. 'She's safe, and at last Felix's dream has come true,' she said. 'He's got Prima in his arms.'

'I don't think this is quite the way he imagined it, though,' I said.

By now, lots of other people had gathered at the railing. Some soldiers threw down a long rope attached to a large cork float that narrowly missed Felix's head as it landed in the water. Felix helped Prima to grab the float, and the soldiers pulled her back on board. Livia, who had just seen what was happening, raced over and hugged and kissed Prima and wrapped her shawl over her shoulders.

The soldiers then rescued Felix, hauling him over the side of the boat like an oversized fish. He sat on the deck, dripping and spluttering. Livia threw herself on her knees in front of him and tried to kiss his hands. Some of the crowd clapped and cheered and slapped him on the back. Felix looked embarrassed.

Suddenly there was a loud whistle. Sailors unwound the heavy ropes that were holding the boat against the harbour wall. I took a last look back to the shore. I knew I would never see anything like this again – and if I lived to tell the tale, I wanted to be able to tell it properly. It was still the middle of the day, but the cloud of smoke and ash made it seem almost dark. I couldn't see Prima's house, or any of the beautiful places where I'd spent the last few days.

Then, with a loud fluttering of its sails, the vessel pushed off and we sailed away from Pompeii and Vesuvius.

21

The boat sailed along the coast, and soon we escaped the foul-smelling cloud. Ash stopped landing on us and the water became calm. We sailed round a bend, and it was almost like Pompeii and the volcano didn't exist any more. The sun was shining, and on the shore, life seemed to be going on as normal.

On board, some people near us were crying and looking back to where they had come from. I wondered if they had lost friends and family, or if they had any idea how great the devastation behind us was going to be.

I found a quiet corner of the deck, and Tilly and I sat down together. I took Saturn out of the schoolbag and cuddled him in my arms. He fell asleep instantly, like all the excitement had been too much for him.

'That was so brave of you, Tilly,' I said.

Tilly shrugged. 'I only took my shoes off,' she said.

'Well, even that was brave. Have you washed your socks lately?'

She giggled. 'I think a slave did it for me. But seriously, I really didn't do anything brave in the end.'

'But you would have,' I said. 'And that's what counts.'

Tilly looked embarrassed.

'Is this what we get for saying life around here is boring?' she asked.

'Maybe. If so, I'm sorry. Give me boring any day. That whole thing was much, much too scary for me. I sooo don't want to end up as a tourist attraction.'

'I wonder where this boat is going?' said Tilly.

'I don't know. They'll probably drop us off somewhere safe and then go back to Pompeii to see if they can save anyone else.'

'And what's going to happen to us when they drop us off?'

'I don't know that either, but Julius and Livia will take care of us, won't they?'

Tilly didn't answer for a long time. Then she said slowly. 'Julius and Livia are good people, but . . .'

'But what?' I asked, half afraid that I knew the answer already.

'Thanks to us, their family survived, but apart from that, they've lost everything. Their beautiful home is probably already buried and won't be seen again for a few thousand years. And . . .'

'And?'

'And they'll have to start all over again. They'll have to sell anything of value.'

'But they've lost all their valuables. We didn't give them time to pack anything, remember? As soon as you grabbed Secunda, they dropped the few things they had gathered.'

'But they haven't lost all their valuables,' said Tilly. 'They've still got us.'

And all of a sudden, I knew she was right.

No matter how nice Julius and Livia were, we were never going to be like family to them. They loved Prima and Secunda, and if selling Tilly and me was going to help them, then that's what would happen. Tilly and I would be back on the onion farm before we knew it.

It was time to go home.

We both looked across to where Prima and her family were huddled round Julius. Felix stood next to them, like a sentry. He looked like he was ready to protect them from any possible harm.

'Do you think they'll have to sell Felix?' asked Tilly.

I shook my head. 'Let's hope not. It would break poor Prima's heart.'

'Should we say goodbye to them before we go?' asked Tilly.

I'd been wondering that too. It seemed mean just to vanish, but how on earth were they ever going to understand?

Even if we spoke the same language, how were they going to understand something as amazing as what we had to say to them?

So I shook my head slowly. 'We saved their lives,'
I said. 'So maybe they'll find it in their hearts to
forgive us for stealing ourselves from them.
Hopefully they won't think too badly of us.'

'They won't,' said Tilly.

'So you're ready?'

Tilly nodded.

'Tell me what you did the last time,' she said.

'I told you. I just held Saturn in my arms and
tried to reason with him.'

'You tried to reason with a cat?'

'I was on a ship that was about to sink. I was
desperate. So I tried to reason with him, and I begged
him, and I threatened him and I stroked him.'

'And which one worked?'

'All of them? None of them? I've no idea. Maybe
the whole thing was just coincidence. All I know is, I
got back home and I was so glad to be there, I didn't
waste too much time wondering about the details.'

'So we'll just do what you did and see what
happens?'

I nodded.

'We'd better do this properly then,' said Tilly. 'I so don't want to be left here on my own. I need to be touching you, I suppose?'

I nodded again. 'I think so. That's probably how you ended up here in the first place. And you'd better put your schoolbag on your back, if you don't want to be in a lot of trouble on Monday morning.'

The two of us huddled together, and I shook Saturn gently to wake him. I held him up in front of me, like a big hairy baby.

He opened his odd eyes and stared at me.

'This is important, Saturn,' I said. 'Remember the last time you and I were on a ship together? Remember how scary that was? Well, Tilly and I think things are going to get scary around here too, and we'd really, really love it if you could find a way to bring us home.'

Saturn blinked once, but nothing happened. We were still on the gently rocking boat, off the coast of Italy.

'Begging isn't working,' said Tilly. 'Try threatening him.'

I put on my crossest face.

'If you don't get us back home, Saturn, Tilly and I are going to be sold. And we got lucky last time, but I don't think we'll find another place where slaves are allowed to have pets. You'll be on your own. You'll probably have to fend for yourself. And as far as I know, you've never caught a mouse in your whole life.'

'He caught a dormouse,' said Tilly.

'It doesn't count if it's dead already. And stop interrupting, Tilly. This is important. Anyway, Saturn, as I was saying, you'll have to fend for yourself and you won't like that, I promise.'

Saturn blinked once more, and once more nothing happened.

'Try stroking him,' said Tilly. 'Maybe that's what did it.'

So I lay Saturn on my lap and stroked him. I stroked his head and his ears. I stroked the soft fur on the side of his face. I stroked his neck and . . .

It worked!

*

I opened my eyes. Tilly and I were sitting on the bench in front of my house. Our tunics had vanished and we were back in our school uniforms. On the grass beside me was my schoolbag, just as I had left it. On the green, Stephen was still kicking a football with his friends.

'Did I just have the most amazing dream?' asked Tilly. 'Or . . .'

'It's the "or",' I said. 'It really happened. We really were in Pompeii.'

'Sorry, Lauren, it's too weird,' said Tilly. 'I can't believe it.'

'Look,' I said, grabbing her wrist. 'We brought back our bangles.'

Tilly gazed at the silver bangle on her arm, but didn't answer.

I rattled my charm bracelet in front of her.

'I brought back the Roman charm,' I said. 'And I left the little silver flower with Prima.'

'OMIGOD,' said Tilly, as the colour drained from her face.

'I know it's totally strange,' I said. 'But you'll get

used to the idea, I promise. Like I said, the first time-travel journey is always the hardest. It's –'

'I believe you, Lauren,' said Tilly. 'I absolutely believe you. It's just that . . .'

She grabbed my arm and pointed.

'I think you should look over there because it seems like we brought back more than a few pieces of jewellery.'

I looked to where Tilly was pointing and I knew that my face was turning chalky white to match hers.

Because sitting on the grass behind the bench, looking very, very confused . . . was Prima.

22

'I saw her on the boat,' said Tilly. 'She was approaching us and holding out her hand. She must have touched me at the last second!'

Prima was getting up and dusting down her tunic. She was looking around her, like nothing made sense any more.

I knew exactly how she felt.

Stephen's friends had stopped playing football and were walking towards us. The cheekiest boy, Nathan, began to laugh.

'Who's your weird friend, Lauren?'

Prima said something in Latin and all the boys started to laugh.

'Sorry,' said Nathan. 'I made a mistake.

I meant, who's your very, very weird friend?'

As he spoke, he reached out and touched Prima's tunic. Prima pulled away and shouted at him.

'She's probably saying that Julius will have him thrown to the lions,' said Tilly. 'Or that she knows an onion farm that's looking for a few extra slaves.'

Prima looked really angry, but the boys continued to laugh at her. I had a horrible feeling that she was going to hit one of them, or pull a sword from under her tunic and try to cut someone's head off.

I knew I had to do something.

'Take your friends away, Stephen,' I said. 'Or I'll tell Dad that it was you who broke the window in the shed.'

Stephen went pale. 'Come on, lads,' he said. 'It's boring here. Let's go back to our game.'

After a few more smart comments, the boys followed him back to the middle of the green.

'Poor Stephen,' said Tilly. 'Are you ever going to tell him that your dad knows about the shed window and doesn't mind because it was an accident?'

I shook my head. 'No way. It's my only method of controlling him.'

Suddenly Prima grabbed my arm and clung on like a limpet. She was shaking and whispering in Latin.

'What is it, Prima?' I said. 'There's nothing to be scared of – well, nothing except for the fact that you've just skipped forward a few thousand years in time.'

'It's the car,' said Tilly. 'She's afraid of the car.'

I hadn't even noticed that a car had driven by. Unfortunately, it was followed by a huge, noisy lorry. Prima began to whimper.

'We have to get her out of here,' I said. 'If a plane flies over, she'll lose her reason altogether.'

'Let's bring her to your place – it's closest,' said Tilly.

'But what will we say to my mum? I think she might notice that Prima isn't one of my usual schoolfriends.'

'Maybe we won't have to tell your mum anything,' said Tilly. 'Maybe we could hide Prima in your bedroom, like the girls did in that Alice and Megan book we read at school.'

'That was a story,' I said. 'That sooo wouldn't work in real life.'

'And your better idea is?'

Of course I didn't have a better idea, so we crossed the road and headed for my house. We let ourselves in through the back door and were tiptoeing up the stairs when Mum heard us.

'Is that you, Lauren?' she said.

I left Tilly and Prima on the stairs and went into the kitchen. Mum was sitting at the table, ready for a long chat.

'So, Lauren,' she said. 'Did you do anything interesting today?'

You mean besides getting sold as a slave (twice), living in an Ancient Roman villa and getting rained on by Vesuvius?

'No. Not really,' I said.

'Well, I had a lovely day. First I watched that great new reality show, and then I –'

'Sorry, Mum,' I said. 'Can we talk later? I have to get something from my bedroom for Tilly.'

Usually, that's the end of that, but for some reason Mum followed me into the hall, where Tilly and Prima were still standing on the stairs.

So much for Tilly's amazing plan.

'Oh, you've got friends with you,' said Mum. 'Hello, Tilly. How are you?'

Tilly beamed at her. 'Hi, Deirdre. I'm good, thanks. And how –'

Before she could finish, Mum had stepped towards Prima.

I was glad that the neck of Prima's tunic covered the flower charm that I had given her. I wasn't so sure any more that my mum would understand why I'd given it away.

'And who's this?' Mum asked. 'I haven't met you before, have I?'

'Oh,' I said quickly. 'This is Prima – Tilly's exchange student. She arrived this morning.'

'That's funny,' said Mum. 'I met your dad yesterday, Tilly. And he didn't mention that you were expecting a visitor.'

'Oh, you know my dad,' said Tilly vaguely.

'And where is Prima from?'

'Slovakia,' I said, saying the first faraway country I could think of.

'Italy,' Tilly said at the same time.

'Kind of on the border between the two,' I said.

I knew from the way that Tilly stared at me that Italy and Slovakia mustn't have a common border, but luckily my mum isn't great at geography, so she didn't notice our mistake.

'So are you all staying for dinner?' asked Mum.

I wasn't at all sure that was a good idea, but before I could answer, Tilly was smiling at Mum again.

'Sure, Deirdre. That would be lovely, thanks.'

Mum went back into the kitchen and the rest of us went on upstairs to my bedroom.

'Why were you still on the stairs?' I said to Tilly. 'It's like you were just waiting to be caught.'

Tilly rolled her eyes and looked at Prima.

'We made slow progress,' she said. 'First Prima had to feel the stair carpet. Then she had to feel the wallpaper. Then she had to smell the paint on the banisters. And when we got to the window on the stairs, she lost the run of herself completely. Who'd have thought that the sight of your neighbour mowing his lawn would be so exciting?'

I giggled. 'The poor girl,' I said. 'Everything must seem so strange.'

'Everything was strange for us in Roman times,' said Tilly.

'Yeah, but it's worse for Prima. At least we've read bits and pieces of our history books. We have the benefit of knowing something about what happened before our time. But the future is a whole different thing. If you and I went to the future, we'd find it a bit weird too.'

'Hey,' said Tilly. 'Do you think Saturn could take us to the future? That would be totally cool.'

'One thing at a time,' I said. 'Maybe we'd better finish with our trip to the past first.'

There was a sudden crash and I turned to see Prima pouncing on the jar of colouring pencils on my desk. She was beaming like she'd just discovered gold.

While Prima was lying on the floor, scribbling all over an old colouring book of Stephen's, I got Mum's laptop, and Tilly and I searched for information about Pompeii.

'OMIGOD!' Tilly gasped. 'Vesuvius erupted in the year 79. We went back almost two thousand years, Lauren! Even thinking about that makes my head hurt.'

I clicked another link and a series of photographs popped up.

'Pompeii's in ruins,' said Tilly.

'What did you expect?'

She sighed. 'I knew that it was ruined, but it's still so weird seeing it. I can't believe we were there just a few minutes ago.'

I tilted the laptop screen, making sure that Prima couldn't see what we were looking at.

How would she feel if she could see her beautiful city so badly damaged?

Tilly and I searched all the pictures, looking in vain for familiar streets.

'It's all so . . . ruined,' I said in the end.

Then Tilly giggled. 'I wish we'd planted my maths book in one of the buildings. Imagine how that would have confused the archaeologists when it was uncovered.'

'I don't know about you,' I said. 'But I was too busy saving my life to think of something like that.'

But speaking of saving lives made me feel sad. I thought of Marca and all of the other slaves on the onion farm. Had they managed to escape? I would never know.

23

When Amy came in for dinner, she looked at Prima's clothes for a long time. She didn't say anything, but my big sister is very easy to read. I knew she was afraid that Roman tunics were an amazing new fashion statement that had somehow managed to pass her by.

Then she looked down at Prima's feet.

'OMG,' she said. 'Those are the most amazing gladiator sandals I've ever seen. Where did you get them? I'd love a pair like that!'

'Prima doesn't speak English,' said Tilly quickly. 'And you can't get sandals like that. The shop she got them in closed down.'

'Ages ago,' I added helpfully.

Amy immediately lost interest in Prima. She went over to the dresser and turned on the radio. Prima ran over and looked round the back of the radio, like she expected to see a group of miniature slaves trapped inside, singing at the tops of their voices.

'She's probably looking for Felix,' said Tilly.

Before I could answer, the microwave pinged and Prima jumped, then collapsed into a loud fit of giggling.

We all sat down and Mum served the food. Prima watched how we used our knives and forks and did her best to copy us, but this wasn't a great success. (It was spaghetti bolognaise for dinner – not easy for a beginner.)

'Poor Prima,' whispered Tilly. 'Imagine, she's from Italy and this is her first time seeing spaghetti.'

When she'd finally managed to empty her plate, Prima leaned over to the salad bowl and picked out a cherry tomato. She smelled it and then she rolled it along the table, like it was a toy.

'Surely she's seen a tomato before?' whispered Tilly.

'Now that I think about it, I didn't see any

tomatoes in Roman times,' I whispered back. 'Maybe they weren't discovered back then.'

Suddenly Prima squeezed the tomato and it burst, spraying Dad with juice and seeds. Prima threw her head back and laughed for ages.

'You'd think that was the funniest thing she'd ever seen,' said Tilly.

'It probably *is* the funniest thing she's ever seen,' I said. 'She's led a very sheltered life.'

Then we were distracted as Prima used the tablecloth to wipe her face and her fingers and the front of her tunic.

While all this was happening, Mum looked vaguely shocked, Stephen giggled at everything Prima did, and Amy paid no attention to anything, as she was too busy fiddling with her iPod.

Dad tried to speak to Prima in every language he knew a few words of. (Luckily he didn't know any Latin.)

Then, when Prima didn't reply to any of his questions, he decided that shouting at her in bad English was the best way to proceed.

'YOU . . . LIKE . . . IRELAND . . . NO?' he screamed. 'IS . . . VERY . . . NICE . . . HERE . . . NO?'

Prima sat back in her chair, looking terrified, but Dad didn't notice. He kept on shouting at her, until Mum patted his arm.

'The poor girl doesn't understand,' she said. 'And I think you might be scaring her a little bit.'

Dad took that as a sign to shout even more loudly and slowly.

'I . . . DID . . . NOT . . . MEAN . . . TO . . . SCARE . . . YOU,' he shouted, so loudly that Prima burst into tears.

She jumped up from the table and ran towards the door. Unfortunately she was still holding the edge of the tablecloth. Stephen grabbed for the other end, but was a second too late. There was a huge crash and soon the floor was a mess of broken dishes and scraps of bolognaise sauce. A single unbroken glass rolled slowly backwards and forwards against the leg of the table before coming to rest at Mum's feet.

Prima stopped at the door and stood there like an Ancient Roman statue.

Amy shrieked.

Stephen said 'Wow!'

Mum was white-faced and speechless.

Dad shrugged and said, 'What did I do?'

Tilly grabbed my arm. 'Looks like a volcano has erupted in your kitchen,' she whispered. It was funny, but one look at Mum's face told me that laughing sooo wouldn't be a good idea.

As soon as we'd all recovered a bit, Mum rushed me out of the room.

'No need for you to help with the clear-up, Lauren,' she said. 'Just take that very strange girl out of here before she does any more weird stuff. I don't care what country she's from, they must be very uncivilized there.'

'Mrs Simms says the Ancient Romans had one of the first great civilizations,' Tilly muttered to me as we each took one of Prima's arms and led her upstairs.

Up in my bedroom, Prima lay on the floor,

drawing all over my English exercise book with my colouring pencils. She didn't seem too bothered that she'd just trashed my kitchen – maybe she thought we had a team of slaves to clean it up again.

'What are we supposed to do with her now?' I asked.

Tilly shrugged. 'I have no idea. And I don't think there are any support groups on the Internet for people who are landed with unexpected visitors from ancient times. Looks like we're on our own.'

'It's getting late, so she'll have to sleep here,' I said. 'And do you think your dad will let you stay over too?'

'But I haven't seen Dad for ages,' protested Tilly. 'It's been days and days.'

I sighed. 'I know it feels like that, but in real time, you saw him just this morning.'

'But –' she began, before I cut her off.

'I really, really want you to stay. I don't think I could face a night here with just Prima and me.'

And so, because Tilly's a good friend, she ran

home and got some overnight stuff. Prima changed into a pair of my pyjamas, and when Tilly got back, she was sitting on my bed, brushing her hair.

'OMIGOD,' said Tilly. 'Prima looks normal. She looks just like one of us.'

I looked at Prima and saw that Tilly was right. Prima wasn't a weirdo from another time and place any more. She looked like an ordinary girl, on an ordinary sleepover. She smiled and I felt a sudden rush of warmth for her. I ran over and hugged her.

'Friends forever,' I said.

Of course Prima didn't understand, but she hugged me back and that was enough.

24

In the morning, Tilly nudged me awake. She pointed at Prima, who was snoring soundly.

'This is so totally weird,' she said. 'Prima belongs thousands of years ago. She probably died thousands of years ago, and yet here she is, alive and well and sleeping on your spare mattress.'

I shrugged. 'Time travel is like that. You and I belong now, and yet we still managed to go back to Ancient Roman times. I was on the *Titanic*, even though it sank long before I was born.'

'Like I said – totally weird.'

Just then, Prima woke up. She sat up and covered her ears, looking absolutely terrified.

From Amy's room, I could hear loud music; from

Stephen's room came the sound of car crashes, courtesy of his latest computer game; downstairs the vacuum cleaner and the coffee maker were competing to see which could have the most irritating sound.

'I never realized what a noisy world we live in,' said Tilly.

I closed my bedroom door, blocking out some of the noise and Prima relaxed a bit.

'I'm starving,' said Tilly suddenly. 'Half my dinner went on the floor last night when Prima did her circus act.'

I was hungry too, but there was no way I was risking another family meal disaster. In the end, I ran downstairs and got some cereal and milk and bowls.

When I got back to my room, I filled each bowl with cereal and Tilly poured in the milk. Beside us, Prima shrieked with laughter.

'What's so funny about cereal?' I wondered before I noticed that Prima was holding her bowl to her ear and listening to the cereal crackling.

'Wouldn't you love to know what's going on inside her head?' I said.

'I'm not sure I could cope with that,' said Tilly.

I laughed. 'Seriously, though, Tilly. Think about it. When we were in Pompeii, we'd have given anything to be able to talk to Prima, but there was no way we could manage it. And now . . .'

'And now you've just become fluent in Latin?'

I sighed. 'Of course not. But lots of people nowadays speak Latin.'

'Like who?'

'Well . . . surely we could find someone. We could ask my parents.'

'OK,' she said doubtfully.

'Think about it,' I said. 'Prima can't stay here forever. Sooner or later, she'll have to go back home to her family.'

'And how exactly are we going to manage that?'

'Let's worry about that later. For now, though, while Prima's here, we have to make the most of it. She's our friend. We have to talk to her . . . get to know her properly.'

Tilly sighed. 'I don't know if you're right,' she said. 'But after a night of listening to Prima sleep-talking in Latin, I haven't got the energy to argue with you.'

'Great,' I said. 'We have a plan. Sort of.'

While Tilly and I got dressed, Prima sat at my mirror and began to fix her hair. She piled it up on her head in a very fashionable way – very fashionable a few thousand years earlier, that is.

Then she found a marker and used it to paint her lips in a gross purply-red colour. With a pink marker, she drew a wobbly circle on each cheek. She smiled at us, and Tilly had to turn away to hide her giggles. Prima looked like someone from a very weird, very low-budget horror movie.

'It's not her fault,' I said. 'She's used to having slaves to make up her face and do her hair.'

'That's true,' said Tilly. 'And maybe we can ignore the face paint, but if we're ever going to go outside this room, we'll have to do something about Prima's clothes.'

She was right. Apart from being totally out of place, Prima's long tunic had been ruined by the mad dash down the hill and the dip in the ocean. Tilly picked it up from the floor and held it in the air. It was crumpled, torn and dirty.

'Why is this still here?' she said. 'The slaves in this place must be very lazy.'

I giggled, and then she continued.

'Prima lent us clothes when we were in Pompeii, so maybe you can give her something to wear,' she suggested.

I opened my wardrobe door and Prima ran over to see what was inside. She ignored my clothes, though, and concentrated on the photographs of Tilly and me that were stuck to the inside of the door. She gazed at each one, and then gazed at Tilly and me, and babbled away in Latin.

'I wonder what's the Latin for "We're going to be here all day"?' sighed Tilly.

We made Prima sit on the bed and we held up loads of clothes for her to choose from, but she shook her head at everything.

'I think it's the trousers that she doesn't like,' said Tilly in the end. 'We didn't see any women wearing trousers in Pompeii, did we?'

'We didn't see any men wearing them either,' I laughed.

'Good point,' said Tilly. 'Looks like you'll have to give her a skirt.'

'I'd love to,' I said, 'if I actually owned one.'

'But you do,' said Tilly, grinning. 'And I know the perfect T-shirt to go with it.'

Soon Prima was dressed. She seemed very pleased with herself in my school skirt and the T-shirt Tilly had chosen for her, which said 21ST CENTURY GIRL across the front in huge black letters.

'Are we ready for the outside world?' asked Tilly.

'I'm not sure the outside world is ready for us,' I muttered. 'But I'll go crazy if I have to stay here any longer.'

'I'll take that as a yes,' said Tilly. 'So let's go.'

25

We met Mum at the bottom of the stairs. She looked at Prima's fancy hairdo and her purple lips; she looked at my school skirt, which was all wrinkled, and much too big for Prima; she watched as Prima picked up the telephone and pressed the buttons, giggling every time they beeped.

'Since this is an exchange, are you going to visit Prima's home, Tilly?' Mum asked. 'If so, I think maybe you should be prepared for an eventful trip.'

'Oh, I've been there already,' said Tilly. 'Just for a few days. Trust me, it was a once-in-a-lifetime experience.'

Mum looked at her in surprise. 'Lauren never mentioned that you'd been away.'

'Oh, well, it was kind of a last-minute thing,' said Tilly vaguely.

'Anyway, Mum,' I said, changing the subject quickly. 'Do you happen to know anyone who speaks Latin?'

Mum put on her dreamy face. 'Yes, I do, actually,' she said. 'There was this boy I knew in college. Very good-looking he was, with long curly hair and the most amazing crinkly blue eyes. He studied Latin. He was always going on about it being the basis for so many European languages. He said –'

'And do you know where he is now?' I interrupted her.

'I know exactly where he is,' said Mum. 'He moved to Borneo with a girl who was studying Greek. I hear they lived happily ever after.'

Tilly sighed. 'So do you know anyone who speaks Latin and lives around here?'

Mum shook her head. 'Sorry. Even in my day, Latin was becoming less popular. In my parents' time more people studied it, especially those who wanted to become doctors. For them it was almost essential. They had to –'

Just then, Prima spotted Mum and Dad's wedding photo, which was hanging next to the front door. She looked at Mum's weird dress and Dad's freaky hair and laughed out loud. I agreed with her that it was totally funny, but something in Mum's face told me that she didn't get the joke.

'We're going out for a while,' I said quickly. 'Is that OK?'

On Saturday mornings, Mum usually makes me do loads of boring jobs in the house, but now she just nodded. She seemed almost glad to be rid of us.

'Thanks for letting me stay over, Deirdre,' said Tilly.

Then we grabbed Prima's arms and raced out the door.

We sat on the bench outside my house. Tilly was grinning and looking very pleased with herself.

'What?' I said.

'I know someone who will definitely speak Latin,' she said.

'Who?' I asked.

'Remember when I did my social-work badge for Guides? We all had to visit an old person and chat to them, and I got that ancient old guy who used to be a doctor. If your mum's right, he'll definitely speak Latin.'

I sighed. 'According to my mum, she's always right.'

'Well, let's hope that on this occasion it's true.'

Then I remembered something else. 'Didn't you say that the man you used to visit was a bit confused? That he's always forgetting stuff and mixing up the present and the past?'

Tilly nodded. 'That's why he's perfect. He won't think it's odd that we're hanging out with a Latin-speaking stray from a few thousand years ago. We can ask him anything we like, and he'll just answer us without all that questioning stuff that adults usually go on with.'

What she said made a weird kind of sense, so we took Prima by the arm and set off for the old man's house.

We made very slow progress.

When we passed the local shop, Prima pressed her nose to the window and stared inside like it was a treasure trove. When we came to the pedestrian crossing, we had to cross the road ten times, while Prima waved at all the motorists, like she was a visiting queen.

'I think I know why farmers put blinkers and earplugs on their horses,' muttered Tilly as we tried to stop Prima running after a little boy on a tricycle.

At last we got to the old man's house. His wife, Kathleen, answered the door and luckily she recognized Tilly.

'You're the nice girl from the Guides,' she said. 'Are you doing another project?'

Tilly nodded. 'Sort of, and this time I've brought my friends. I hope that's OK?'

Kathleen didn't answer. Instead she looked at Prima with her painted face and badly fitting clothes.

'This is Prima,' said Tilly. 'She's on her way to a fancy-dress party.'

Kathleen smiled. 'With you young people, sometimes it's hard to tell.'

Tilly and I laughed politely, while Prima pressed repeatedly on the doorbell, clapping her hands in time with its chiming.

Kathleen led us inside, ignoring Prima's weird behaviour.

'Patrick likes company,' she said. 'And if you chat to him, I can get on with my ironing. I hope he won't bore you too much, though.'

'Why would he bore us?' asked Tilly.

'Oh, surely you remember from your last visit? Patrick loves to talk about the olden days, and that can't be of any interest to young people like you.'

Tilly smiled sweetly. 'Don't you worry about us,' she said. 'We love to talk about olden times, don't we, Lauren?'

I smiled an even sweeter smile. 'The older the better,' I said.

 **26**

Patrick was sitting in a big leather armchair in a study at the back of the house. He didn't remember Tilly, and didn't seem to mind that she was visiting him with two strangers – one of whom was very, very strange.

'I'll leave you to it,' said Kathleen. 'Just call if you need anything.'

Then she went off to do her ironing.

'These are my friends, Lauren and Prima,' said Tilly to Patrick.

Patrick smiled. 'Prima is an interesting name,' he said. 'If she lived in Roman times, it would mean she was the eldest daughter in the family. All first-born girls were called Prima.'

'Like Prima Donna or Prima Ballerina,' said Tilly.

Patrick nodded. 'And the second born was called –'

'Secunda!' said Tilly and I together.

'Why didn't we figure that out before?' said Tilly.

'Maybe because we had other stuff on our minds – like staying alive,' I replied.

'And it goes on from there,' said Patrick. '*Tertia, Quarta, Quinta, Sexta, Septima, Octava, Nona, Decima* . . .'

'Sounds a bit boring to me,' I said.

'Sounds totally confusing to me,' said Tilly. 'Imagine what it must be like at school? The teacher says, 'Is Prima here today?' and half the girls in the class put up their hands.'

Patrick laughed. 'Not exactly. Outside the family, girls were known by their fathers' names.'

'I'm glad I live now,' I said suddenly.

'Me too,' said Tilly.

'I think your friend is happy as well,' said Patrick, smiling.

We both looked at Prima. She was twirling on a

revolving chair and waving her arms madly in the air.

Then Patrick launched into a long story about how he got into trouble for stealing sweets decades earlier. As soon as he stopped for breath, Tilly interrupted him.

'Er, Patrick, do you speak Latin?' she asked.

He smiled at her. 'Of course I do. Studied it for seven years. Or was it six? No, I think it was seven. Now let me see. Old Mr Lucas taught me for two years, and then he got gallstones – very painful – so he was replaced by Mr Ryan. I didn't like Mr Ryan very much. One day he . . .'

Patrick rambled on and on, giving us every single boring detail about something his teacher did to him, way back when the Second World War was still being fought.

'The poor man,' Tilly whispered to me. 'He can't remember what happened yesterday and yet all that ancient stuff is fresh in his mind.'

'Let's hope Latin is still fresh in his mind too,' I whispered back.

As soon as Patrick got to the end of his tale, Tilly sat Prima on the couch in front of him.

'Our friend speaks Latin too,' she said. 'Maybe you could have a chat.'

Patrick said something in Latin, and a slow smile spread over Prima's face. Then she spoke back to him, rambling on for ages and ages.

'Wow,' said Tilly. 'It works.'

'What did she say?' I asked.

Patrick patted Prima's arm. 'Your friend speaks perfect Latin,' he said. 'But she seems a bit confused, the poor little thing.'

'Takes one to know one,' whispered Tilly to me.

'But what did she say?' I asked again.

Patrick scratched his head. 'She said lots of things. It's almost as if she's bursting to talk.'

I felt a sudden flash of pity for Prima. The whole volcano thing was scary enough, without getting dragged into the future where no one could understand her – until now.

'She said something about a boat,' said Patrick. 'And a volcano. She said her father hurt his leg and that she fell in the water. She said she's lost now and misses her family very much.'

I went over and put my arm round Prima, and she squeezed my hand.

'OMG,' said Tilly. 'They can really understand each other. This is totally amazing. What should we ask her?'

I thought back to our trip to Pompeii and all the things I'd wanted to ask Prima, but couldn't. I thought of all the days when I would have given anything to be able to communicate with her. Now, though, my mind had gone blank.

Tilly seemed the same. 'We could ask what her favourite colour is,' she said in the end.

'That's a bit pathetic,' I said. 'And anyway, I know that already. Prima's favourite colour is green. I've noticed that she always takes the green first when she sees our colouring pencils.'

'We could ask her if they really were dormice they were serving for dinner each night,' suggested Tilly.

I shuddered. 'I sooo don't want to know the answer to that question.'

Then I had an idea. I turned to Patrick.

'Could you please ask her who we are?'

He nodded and said something in Latin, and Prima quickly replied.

The doctor tried not to smile. 'Dear me,' he said. 'Your poor little friend really is confused.'

'So what did she say?' I asked.

'She says you are her slaves, but I shouldn't be worried as you are well educated and healthy and that you don't have lice.'

'How dare she?' said Tilly angrily. 'Doesn't she know –'

Before she could finish, Prima added something else.

'And she says you are true and loyal friends too,' translated Patrick.

Then I thought of something else. 'Can you ask her why her father bought us, please?'

'Remember, he only bought you,' said Tilly. 'He stole me.'

I laughed. 'Whatever,' I said. 'Just let the man talk.'

195

Once again the doctor had a half-smile on his face as he spoke to Prima and then translated.

'She says that she was sad because her favourite dog had died, and her father bought you to make her feel better.'

Now Tilly was really, really cross.

'Julius bought us to replace a dog? He used us like toys to console a spoiled child. We're human beings. How could he treat us like that? I thought we were part of his family.'

I patted her arm. 'Times were different then,' I said. 'Julius and Prima were brought up with the idea of slavery – with the idea of buying and selling people. They didn't know any better.'

Soon Tilly calmed down – luckily she really doesn't know how to hold a grudge.

We chatted with Prima for ages and after a while, it didn't feel weird to have Patrick sitting between us, translating everything we said.

Patrick didn't seem to think it was strange that Prima spoke such perfect Latin and acted like she belonged in a different age. Or that the three of us were totally engrossed in a conversation that really shouldn't make any sense at all.

Now that we could communicate properly, Tilly and I could see that Prima was sweet and funny. She was worried about her family, and the volcano, but she seemed to believe us when we told her that we'd get her back home safely. (And conveniently she didn't ask us to explain how exactly we were going to manage that.)

After a while, Kathleen came in with a tray of lemonade and biscuits.

'I can see you're all having a lovely time here,' she said, as she handed out the glasses. 'But maybe it's best if you just stay for another fifteen minutes or so. Patrick gets tired easily.'

'Sure thing,' said Tilly.

Then she turned to me and whispered. 'But I'm not leaving here until I get the answer to one last question.'

27

I had a fair idea that I knew what was on Tilly's mind, and it turned out that I was right.

'Please, Patrick,' she said. 'Could you ask Prima if she thinks Felix is hot?'

Patrick looked worried. 'Is Felix a friend of yours? If he has a high temperature, he might need to see a doctor.'

Tilly giggled. 'I didn't mean that kind of hot. I meant, could you please ask her if she likes Felix?'

'Oh, you young people and your obsession with love,' sighed Patrick.

Then he said something to Prima. Tilly nudged me as we both recognized the word 'Felix'.

Before answering, Prima sipped her lemonade for

the first time. She almost dropped the glass when some bubbles went up her nose.

Patrick patted her on the back until she had stopped coughing, and then he repeated the question. Prima was blushing as she replied.

Patrick quickly translated. 'She says Felix is a loyal slave, with good teeth and a strong back.'

'That's a bit vague,' said Tilly. 'She might as well be talking about a horse.'

I knew we had to get to the point.

'Please ask her if she'd like to marry him,' I said.

Prima was quick to answer and the doctor translated. 'She says Felix would make a fine husband.'

'Yessss!' said Tilly, before Patrick continued.

'But her father would never allow her to marry a slave. Her father will choose her a suitable husband of noble birth.'

'Nooo!' said Tilly.

'You'd think they were living in the Dark Ages,' I said.

Tilly giggled. 'I think the Dark Ages came after Ancient Roman times.'

'Who cares about minor details like that?' I said. 'We have to do something to help Prima. She's our friend. She saved you from the wolves and me from the onion farm. We can't abandon her to a miserable life of sitting at home doing embroidery and playing really awful music.'

'But we can't change any of that. That's the Roman way of life.'

'I know, but if Prima was married to someone she actually loved, then surely that would make all the difference? She'd be happy and she might manage not to die of boredom.'

'But you heard what she said. Her father won't allow her to marry a slave.'

'Maybe there's something we can do about that,' I said.

'But . . .'

I grinned. At last I knew something about history that Tilly didn't.

'Felix doesn't have to be a slave forever,' I said. 'A master can grant a slave his freedom, and then he'd be free to marry anyone he wants.'

'But what can we do to make that happen? I don't fancy going back to Pompeii again, and even if we did, how could we explain to Julius?'

Then she giggled. 'I don't suppose we could persuade Patrick to hop back to ancient times for a few minutes?' she said. 'Julius would listen to him, I bet.'

I giggled too, glad that Patrick was busy polishing his glasses, and paying no attention to our conversation.

'Yeah,' I said, 'but would Patrick remember the message? He'd probably get distracted and try to tell Julius a long story about his Latin teacher's sister's ingrown toenail, or something irrelevant like that.'

Suddenly I had an idea. 'Remember how Julius used to get loads of letters every day?'

Tilly grinned. 'How could I forget? That messenger boy was totally cute.'

I rolled my eyes. 'Forget the messenger boy and remember how seriously Julius took those letters.'

Tilly nodded. 'I remember.'

'Well, we could get Patrick to write Julius a letter,'

I said. 'We could make it all official-looking, and Prima could take it back to her father. Maybe he'd do as the letter suggested. Maybe –'

'Hang on a sec. Have we figured out how Prima's going to get back to her father yet?'

'Er . . . no. But that's not important right now. Let's get the letter written and we can worry about the other details later.'

Much later, Patrick held up the letter.

'It was very nice to write the old language,' he said. 'It's like being back in university again. I wrote exactly what you said. Will I read it back to you?'

Tilly and I nodded and he began, translating into English as he read.

Dear Titus Julius Arcanus,

It has come to my attention that your slave Felix has done some wonderful things lately. He saved your life when you hurt your leg, and then he jumped into the sea and saved your daughter's life too. I am just an interested observer, but

I would suggest that your slave Felix has earned his
freedom. I would also suggest that you could reward him
by letting him marry your daughter. You don't have to do
what I say, but I think you should.

Sincerely,
Doctor Patrick Turner

I took the letter from him and handed it to Prima.
She read it very slowly and then a smile spread
across her face.

'Yay, she's up for it!' said Tilly.

Then Prima said something to Patrick.

'She will give the letter to her father and say it
was written by a very kind, very important man,' he
said, blushing slightly.

Poor Patrick. He probably hadn't felt important
for a very long time.

'I don't suppose you have any sealing wax or
anything?' I said then, remembering the letters that
the messenger used to bring to Julius.

The doctor shook his head and pretended to be

cross. 'I'm not that old, you know, young lady. Sealing wax went out long before my time.'

I didn't want to give up. 'Or an official-looking stamp or something?'

Patrick turned and started to rummage through a drawer in the desk.

'I think there might be some things here from my old surgery. Kathleen always tries to throw them out, but I won't let her. I'm hoping that maybe one day I'll be well enough to practise as a doctor again.'

I felt a sudden rush of pity for the poor old man. He was so kind and helpful, and had no sense of how confused he was.

Then he beamed as he pulled out some old-fashioned rubber stamps.

'Here they are,' he said. 'Now, which one would you like?'

'What do they say?' I asked.

'Hmm, this first one says URINE SAMPLE ENCLOSED.'

Tilly and I giggled. 'That's not really what we had in mind. What else have you got?'

Patrick read the next one. 'PAID WITH THANKS.'

'Perfect,' I said. 'After all, Felix has paid for his freedom twice over.' I folded up the letter and Patrick used red ink to stamp the fold.

Just then Kathleen came in and we knew it was time to leave.

'I think Patrick has really enjoyed your visit,' she said as he stood up and formally shook our hands.

I tried not to feel too guilty as I wondered what his poor confused mind must have made of this whole event. Then we thanked them both and left.

It wasn't lunchtime yet, but already it felt like it had been a very long day.

28

The journey home with Prima took ages and ages. Who'd have thought a bin lorry would be so exciting? Or two toddlers in a double buggy?

When we finally made it to my house, I couldn't face going inside, so we went into the back garden.

Prima amused herself by spinning the rotary washing line in circles and running round after it like a crazy girl.

Tilly and I went and sat on the grass.

'So now what are we going to do?' asked Tilly.

I shrugged. I had absolutely no idea what we were going to do next.

'We're the ones who brought Prima here,' said Tilly. 'So she's our responsibility.'

'I know. But we can't cope with this on our own. It's too big. We'll have to get some help.'

'From whom?'

'From someone who'd believe us when we say, "This is Prima and she's come to visit us from Ancient Rome, and we're wondering if we should send her back. And incidentally, we've just spent a few days being slaves and watching Vesuvius destroying Pompeii. Oh, and by the way, did I mention the magical cat who seems to be part of this whole time-travelling thing?"'

I sighed. 'That sounds totally crazy to me, even though I know for sure it's true.'

'And there's another thing,' said Tilly. 'Even if we did manage to find someone who believed us, they'd probably haul poor Prima off and do scientific experiments on her, like they tried to do with ET.'

'But we have to do something. We can't just keep her here. We've both got hockey practice tonight.'

'And I've got swimming this afternoon. And what about school on Monday?'

I giggled. 'Mrs Simms is always going on about

historical artefacts. What would she say if we brought Prima in for Show and Tell?'

Tilly giggled too. 'That would be so amazing,' she said.

I sighed. 'But you know how formal Mrs Simms is. She'd insist on putting Prima's name on the register. And what would we say when she asked awkward stuff like her date of birth?'

'Or the name of her last school?'

I sighed again. 'Anyway, it wouldn't be fair on Prima. She's worried about her mum and dad and Secunda. And she misses Felix. She's had some excitement here, but it's time for her to go home now.'

'And there's something else too,' said Tilly. 'Remember when Columbus went to America, loads of native Americans died because they couldn't fight the diseases that the explorers had brought with them.'

'So Prima could be at risk from modern diseases?'

Tilly nodded. 'Probably. And we wouldn't want to find out the hard way, would we?'

I knew she was right. There were all kinds of

good reasons for sending Prima back home. All we had to figure out was how to do it.

When we went inside, Mum handed Prima's tunic to her. While we were gone, she had washed and dried and ironed it.

Tilly laughed. 'Prima must think your mum is a slave,' she said to me.

'I heard that, Tilly,' said Mum. 'And you're right, sometimes I do feel like a slave around here.'

'Trust me, Mum,' I said. 'Being a slave is harder than you'd think.'

Before she could answer, Prima began to sniff the tunic and stroke her face with it.

'I think maybe her family uses a different brand of fabric conditioner,' said Tilly.

While Prima changed back into her own clothes, I dug around in my wardrobe for an old rucksack.

'What's that for?' asked Tilly.

'If Prima does manage to get back home, wouldn't it be nice if she brought some presents from the future?' I asked.

'That's a totally brilliant idea,' said Tilly. 'Now let's get Prima out of here so we can do this properly.'

I took Prima out to the back garden and bribed Stephen to keep an eye on her, while she ran around the washing line. Then I went back up to my room.

Tilly was sitting on my bed, holding the empty rucksack.

'This is an amazing opportunity,' she said. 'So we have to think really carefully about what we send back with Prima. Have you any ideas?'

'Maybe we should send her back with a pizza?' I suggested. 'I was really disappointed to learn that they didn't have pizzas in ancient times. Maybe if we don't send one back now, pizza will never be invented – and how tragic would that be?'

'Totally tragic,' said Tilly.

Suddenly I had another idea. I ran into Stephen's room and returned with his talking Buzz Lightyear toy.

'Prima can give this to Felix,' I said. 'I know he's too old for toys, but this would be a huge novelty back in Pompeii. Maybe it would help Felix to impress Julius.'

'I'm not so sure about giving that to Prima,' said Tilly.

'Stephen won't mind,' I said. 'He never plays with it any more.'

'That's not what I meant. It's just that . . . maybe it's against the rules.'

'There are rules? Since when?'

She sighed. 'I don't know. But maybe it's wrong to send something made of plastic back to a time thousands of years before it's been invented.'

She did have a point. While I was thinking about it, I pulled the string on the toy's back and the mechanical voice said '*To infinity and beyond!*'

'When the makers of that toy talked about infinity, they didn't know how right they were,' I said. 'Doesn't it seem kind of appropriate to send it back a few thousand years?'

Tilly shrugged. 'I'm still not sure. But if we ever hear that it was the wrong thing to do, we can go back to the year 79 and pick it up again.'

I shook my head quickly. 'No way. I plan to stay in the twenty-first century for a while, if that's OK with you. Now what else will we put in?'

Before long, the rucksack was full. Inside it were:

the letter to Julius

Buzz Lightyear

a small pizza in a box

a few cherry tomatoes

a big bag of salt and vinegar crisps

a huge packet of colouring pencils

some gel pens

a picture book and a rag doll for Secunda

some embroidery threads I'd found in an old craft
   kit for Livia

'That's the easy part finished,' said Tilly as she zipped up the bag.

'And the hard part is?'

'The hard part is figuring out how exactly we're going to get Prima and all this stuff back to Ancient Pompeii.'

 29

When we got back to the garden, Prima had stopped chasing the washing in circles. Now she was running up and down the small plastic slide that Stephen had stopped playing on years earlier. Stephen was very glad to see us.

'I don't care if you tell Dad about the shed window,' he said. 'Just don't ever ask me to mind Prima again. It's too scary.'

Suddenly I felt sorry for him. 'Dad knows about the shed window,' I said. 'He doesn't mind.'

At first Stephen looked relieved, before he realized that I'd been tricking him for months. He was getting ready to scream at me when Tilly stepped in.

'If you're not busy, Stephen, would you just wait here with Prima for another few minutes? Lauren and I have to –'

Before she could finish, Stephen had raced inside, slamming the back door behind him. I knew exactly how he felt.

Tilly and I sat on the grass.

'All we have to do is persuade Saturn to take Prima back home,' said Tilly, like that was the easiest thing in the world.

I was still very worried.

'We have no real idea how this whole time-travel stuff works,' I said. 'Even if we manage to persuade Saturn to whisk Prima away from here, that might not be the right way to go. How can we trust him to take her to the right time and place? She could end up on the *Titanic* like I did – and she wouldn't know what a disaster that turned out to be.'

'But –'

I didn't let her finish. 'What if Prima gets lost in time and she's all on her own?' I said. 'Maybe we should go with her just in case?'

Tilly shook her head. 'It's not like we've known Prima forever, is it?'

'It feels like we've known her forever,' I said. 'We've been through a lot together.'

'I know what you mean,' said Tilly. 'But I think there's a better chance of Saturn taking Prima back to her own place and time if we're not there to distract him.'

'That's true,' I said. 'But there's one other thing – even if Saturn gets Prima home to Pompeii, how is he going to get back here to us afterwards?'

Tilly hugged me. 'We can't be sure he will. We'll just have to hope.'

She had a point. I couldn't imagine what I would do if I lost Saturn, but for Prima's sake, I had to be brave.

So I left Tilly to sort Prima out while I went inside to look for my unsuspecting pet.

A few minutes later, Prima was sitting in the middle of our lawn with my old rucksack on her back and Saturn in her arms. Prima was staring at us, like she knew that something important was going to happen. I wanted to hug her, but I didn't dare.

'Friends forever?' I said.

'Friends . . . forever,' she repeated slowly, and then she smiled at me almost like she understood.

Tilly and I were sitting nearby, careful not to touch any part of Prima or Saturn or the rucksack. I was sooo tempted to reach out and stroke Saturn's soft fur, but I knew that would be a really, really bad idea.

I picked up the paper and pencils I'd brought outside with me, and Prima smiled. I drew a picture of a house.

'*Domus*,' I said, using the word Prima had taught us.

Prima thought it was a game. She pointed at my house. '*Domus*,' she said. 'House.'

Tilly shook her head. 'No, Prima,' she said. 'This isn't a language lesson. This is important. We're trying to send you home.'

Of course Prima didn't understand.

I drew three stick figures in the house. 'Julius, Livia, Secunda,' I said, pointing. Then I drew two more – a boy and girl holding hands. 'Felix and Prima,' I said.

Now Prima smiled and nodded.

I gazed at Saturn. 'I know you've done a lot of time-travelling lately, and you must be a bit tired,' I said. 'But this is important. Prima needs to go home, and Tilly and I can't go along, so we're trusting you to take her, OK?'

Saturn blinked and his odd eyes opened wide.

'It's all your fault,' I said. 'You brought her here and you've got to take her back.'

Saturn sat in Prima's arms, looking bored.

'Maybe she should stroke him,' said Tilly, miming a stroking action.

Prima noticed and began to stroke Saturn. For a few minutes nothing happened and I had a horrible feeling that we were wasting our time.

In my mind I was trying to think of a way of integrating Prima into my life forever. I was already trying to figure out how I was going to persuade my parents to adopt this strange, lovely girl, who had appeared out of nowhere.

Then Saturn went rigid. He arched his back and began to tremble.

'It's working,' whispered Tilly. 'And I think I know —'

Before she could finish her sentence, Saturn flicked his tail. As if in slow motion, it arched through the air and touched the side of Tilly's arm.

'Nooo,' I screamed as I threw myself forward and grabbed her other arm.

Then everything seemed to happen at once. Prima and Saturn shimmered and then became transparent, before vanishing completely.

I tried to pull Tilly away, but it was like trying to move a mountain. I watched in horror as her arm and then her body began to shimmer and become transparent.

'No way, Tilly!' I screamed. 'You're not going with them! I'm not letting you go!'

I ground my heels into the grass and pulled like I had never pulled before. The shimmery effect was moving along Tilly's arm towards my desperately clutching fingers. I knew that if I didn't let go soon, I was going to be in big, big trouble.

Then, just when I thought my muscles were going to explode, I tumbled backwards and Tilly – a perfect, solid, non-transparent Tilly – tumbled on top of me.

She began to babble like a crazy thing.

'OMIGOD!' she said. 'That was so amazing, Lauren. Saturn was so clever. He took Prima right back to the boat. I saw Livia and Julius and Felix and everybody, but it was like I was looking at them through frosted glass or something. They didn't seem surprised to see Prima, but she was totally surprised to see them. And she was undoing the rucksack and taking out the letter. And part of me wanted to stay to see that everything turned out OK with the letter for Julius. Part of me wanted to go to Prima and Felix's wedding. But I could feel you pulling me back and I was afraid of being in the past on my own, so I leaned towards you and here I am. But it was all so totally amazing, like being on the weirdest roller coaster ever!'

Then I remembered. 'Before Saturn's tail touched you, you were saying something. You said you knew . . .'

Her eyes lit up. 'Yes, I remember now. I know how it happens. I know how to make Saturn go travelling. It's so obvious, I don't know why we didn't think of it before.'

'So tell me!' I said.

'It's his collar.'

'His collar?'

She nodded. 'I was watching Prima stroking Saturn and nothing was happening, and then her hand brushed his collar. Her fingers ran along the blue and green stones and that's when things started to go crazy.'

I thought back to the *Titanic* and to our recent trip to Pompeii, and I knew that this was the answer. It wasn't Saturn that had the secret powers, it was his collar!

'This is so amazing,' said Tilly. 'Now that we know how to make it happen, we can go time-travelling whenever we want. We can figure out exactly how the stones work. We can go anywhere we want in the past. Maybe we could even go to the future – how cool would that be? And we'd never have to be scared because we could just press the coloured stones and come back whenever we wanted. We could –'

I interrupted her. 'Tilly.'

'What?'

'Where's Saturn?'

We stood up and looked all around, but there was no sign of him.

'He should be back,' I said. 'Even if he stayed for hours, or days in ancient time, he should be back by now.'

'I saw him back in the past,' said Tilly. 'He was on the deck of the boat, right next to Prima.'

I put my face in my hands. 'This is awful,' I said. 'There's no one to press the stones on his collar. He could be stuck there. Forever.'

Tilly and I searched for ages and ages. We searched the garden and the house, and the streets around our house. We persuaded Stephen and his friends to search anywhere they could think of.

Everyone had seen lots of cats, but no one had seen a beautiful fluffy white cat with one blue eye and one green one, wearing a collar studded with magical blue and green stones.

'It's like Saturn has vanished off the face of the earth,' said Tilly, much later.

'In a way, he has,' I said.

It was kind of funny, but neither of us laughed. This sooo wasn't a laughing matter.

'I hope Prima will take good care of him,' I said. 'I won't feel quite so bad about losing him, if I know that he's OK.'

'Of course Prima will take care of him,' she replied. 'And she might even figure out a way of sending him back here to us.'

I shook my head sadly. 'I don't think so,' I said. 'I have a horrible feeling we're never going to see Saturn again.'

Tilly and I finished our history project on Ancient Italy and we got top marks.

'Excellent work, girls. Most authentic,' said Mrs Simms. 'It's almost like you were there. The library is running a competition in conjunction with its history festival, and you should enter. I think your project has a very good chance of winning.'

'Thanks,' muttered Tilly and I together.

'You don't seem very pleased,' said Mrs Simms.

'We are,' I said. 'It's just . . .'

'It's just that we have a lot on our minds right now,' Tilly finished for me. 'Lauren's cat has gone missing.'

Mrs Simms nodded understandingly, but it didn't help. Nothing could help. Tilly and I both loved Saturn and we both missed him very much. And without Saturn, there was one very big question hanging over our lives.

Were our time-travelling days finished forever?

 30

'Why didn't Saturn come back to us?' said Tilly for the hundredth time as we sat in my room one afternoon, looking at a cute photograph of him curled up on my bed. 'I still don't understand it. I thought that no matter how long he spent in the past, he'd be back here in no time at all.'

'That's what I thought too. But maybe I was wrong.'

'Or maybe he left Pompeii and couldn't get right back here. Maybe he's a few miles away and can't find his way home,' said Tilly.

'But I put my mobile number on his collar. Someone would ring me if they found him.'

'But what if he got back to a place where phones aren't invented yet? He could be lost in any time or place in the world and we'd never know it.' Then she looked up and saw the tears in my eyes, so she hugged me and I felt better – for a few short seconds.

Days and days went by.

In my mind, I gave up hope of ever seeing Saturn again. Still, though, every time I went outside, I couldn't help looking for him. I couldn't help waking up in the night, thinking that I'd heard his miaow outside my bedroom window.

But he was never there.

'Let's go to the pet shop, Lauren,' said Mum one day. 'We can pick you out a kitten – any one you want. I know it won't be the same, but . . .'

I shook my head sadly. Mum had no idea how special Saturn had been to me. She had no idea how *special* he was.

Then one afternoon, Tilly and I were sitting in my garden when my phone rang.

'OMIGOD. OMIGOD. OMIGOD,' was all I could say.

By the time I hung up, Tilly was jumping around with excitement. 'It's about Saturn, isn't it?' she said.

I nodded happily.

'A woman all the way up in Donegal found him in a barn on her farm. She said she had no idea how he got there, or how long he's been there. She's going to call back later and we'll have to figure out a way of picking him up.'

Tilly hugged me so tightly I thought that my ribs were going to be crushed, but I didn't care. Saturn was coming home and that was all that mattered!

Dad's cousin's husband's friend is a long-distance truck driver, and the next day, his huge truck pulled up outside our front door.

Tilly and I ran outside just as the driver jumped down from his cab, carrying a large cardboard box with holes cut in the sides.

'Special delivery,' he said, smiling.

I put the box on the ground and opened it carefully.

He was filthy and skinny, and his beautiful fur was all matted, but there was no mistaking those amazing blue and green eyes. My cat was back.

I picked him up and hugged him tightly, not caring that I was ruining my clothes.

'Oh, my baby,' I said. 'Where have you been? *When* have you been? And why has it taken you so long to come back to me?'

Tilly reached out and I handed Saturn to her so she could hug him too.

We ran inside.

Mum, Dad and Stephen hugged Saturn like he was their long-lost child home again. Even Amy looked up and patted Saturn's head, which was a big deal for her.

'We have to feed this poor creature,' said Mum, pulling out the bag of cat food that we kept in the cupboard under the sink.

Saturn devoured his food and I wondered what he'd been eating since I'd last seen him. Had he survived on a diet of flamingos' tongues? Or had he been chasing mice in Donegal?

As soon as Saturn finished eating, Tilly and I took him outside to try to clean him up.

'Better take off his collar,' said Tilly. 'We don't want any strange accidents, do we.'

As I carefully unbuckled the collar, I noticed that there was a tiny leather pouch attached to it.

'OMIGOD!' whispered Tilly. 'What could that be?'

'I have no idea,' I answered. 'And why are you whispering?'

'Because this is so totally amazing,' she whispered. 'Saturn has brought us something from the past. Now open it before I die of suspense!'

I untied the pouch and held it in my hand.

'Does it feel like diamonds or gold?' asked Tilly.

I shook my head. 'No. It's too light.'

'Maybe it's a deep-fried dormouse,' she said.

I shuddered.

'Maybe it's . . .' she began.

Suddenly I couldn't wait any more. With shaking fingers, I loosened the string that was holding the pouch closed.

'What is it?' asked Tilly as I pulled out a piece of folded-up papyrus.

I unfolded the papyrus and saw that there was a message written on it – in bright green colouring pencil.

'It's a letter,' I whispered. 'Prima sent us a letter.'

'What does it say?' asked Tilly.

'It says lots of stuff – but it's all in Latin.'

'This is so totally exciting,' said Tilly. 'This means that Prima figured out that Saturn was the key to all the mad stuff that happened to us. It means that she figured out how to send him back to us. I wonder what she wants to tell us?'

'I hope it isn't the recipe for deep-fried dormouse.'

Tilly giggled. 'Anyway,' she said, 'there's only one way to find out.'

We brought Saturn back inside for Mum to pamper and then Tilly and I set off for Patrick's house.

Kathleen seemed pleased to see us.

'You know, after your last visit, Patrick seemed much brighter and happier in himself,' she said.

'We enjoyed that visit too,' said Tilly. 'Do you think we could see him for a minute? There's something we'd like to ask him.'

'Of course,' said Kathleen. 'But don't be too disappointed if he's forgotten who you are. You know how confused he gets.'

Then she showed us into Patrick's study and left us to it.

Patrick remembered us at once and seemed disappointed that Prima wasn't with us.

'Where's your Latin-speaking friend?' he asked.

'Oh,' said Tilly. 'She's off speaking Latin somewhere. But we have a note she wrote before she left. Do you think you could translate it for us?'

Patrick spent ages looking for his reading glasses and by the time he found them in the middle of a pot plant, Tilly and I were practically jumping up and down with anticipation.

Patrick read the note silently, then smiled to himself. 'What a wonderful imagination your young friend has,' he said. 'She reminds me a lot of my younger sister, Eleanor. Of course Eleanor's not so young now

– she's eighty-seven, or is it eighty-eight? She –'

'Er, Patrick, do you think you could tell us what the note says?' I asked.

He smiled. 'I do go on a bit, don't I?'

We couldn't argue with that, so we said nothing while Patrick resettled his glasses on his nose and began to translate.

Greetings, Lauren and Tilly,

Felix and I are married now. We have twin girls, Prima and Secunda. We live in a humble house with only seven bedrooms and a very small swimming pool, but even so, we are all very happy.

Your friend,
Prima

'OMG,' said Tilly. 'Saturn stayed there for ages and ages. And our plan worked. Everything turned out exactly as we hoped.'

I sighed. 'It's like a fairytale. Prima and Felix got the whole happy-ever-after thing. That is so, so amazing.'

Just then Patrick turned the piece of papyrus over. 'There's more,' he said.

I wasn't sure I wanted to hear more. Prima and Felix were happy and that was all I cared about. But Patrick was already reading aloud.

Postscriptum: Because you helped my family so much, I now grant you your freedom. You are slaves no more.

Patrick handed the letter back to us. 'You girls,' he said, shaking his head.

We thanked him, took the letter and skipped out of the house.

'Free at last,' said Tilly, and we both laughed all the way home.

It all started with a Scarecrow.

Puffin is seventy years old.

Sounds ancient, doesn't it? But Puffin has never been
so lively. We're always on the lookout for the next big
idea, which is how it began all those years ago.

Penguin Books was a big idea from the mind of
a man called Allen Lane, who in 1935 invented
the quality paperback and changed the world.
**And from great Penguins, great Puffins grew,
changing the face of children's books forever.**

The first four Puffin Picture Books were hatched in 1940 and the
first Puffin story book featured a man with broomstick arms called
Worzel Gummidge. In 1967 Kaye Webb, Puffin Editor, started the
Puffin Club, promising to **'make children into readers'.**
She kept that promise and over 200,000 children became
devoted Puffineers through their quarterly instalments of
Puffin Post, which is now back for a new generation.

Many years from now, we hope you'll look back and
remember Puffin with a smile. **No matter what your age
or what you're into, there's a Puffin for everyone.**
The possibilities are endless, but one thing is for sure:
whether it's a picture book or a paperback, a sticker book
or a hardback, **if it's got that little Puffin
on it – it's bound to be good.**